# PLEASANT RIVER

# PLEASANT RIVER

## DALE REX COMAN

*Illustrated by the Author*

**DOWN EAST MAGAZINE**
Camden/Maine

*Reprinted by arrangement with*

*Dale Rex Coman*

COPYRIGHT © 1966 BY W. W. NORTON & COMPANY, INC.

*To*
MONA
CHARITY *and* MICHAEL

# Contents

| 1 | Introducing the Pleasant | 17 |
| --- | --- | --- |
| 2 | From Dawn to Dark | 27 |
| 3 | A Visit to the Narraguagus and Speculations about Circles and Straight Lines | 37 |
| 4 | The New Canoe | 51 |
| 5 | Of Turtles and Teenagers | 61 |
| 6 | June Twenty-second | 69 |
| 7 | Alewives and Daisies, Trout and Harebells | 79 |
| 8 | In July | 87 |
| 9 | When Nothing Much Happens | 97 |
| 10 | Of a Day in Summer | 113 |
| 11 | To the Source of the Pleasant | 127 |
| 12 | Of Toads and Truants, Sinners and Savants | 141 |
| 13 | One of Those Days | 149 |
| 14 | Departure | 163 |

# Acknowledgments

I wish to convey my earnest thanks to those who have, in one way or another, contributed to the production of this book. First, to Mona, my wife, whose gentle prodding launched the project in the first place and whose kindly suggestions have been helpful beyond measure during its development. To Sculley Bradley, who has patiently read and reread the manuscript, whose wise counsel has been invaluable, and whose encouragement prevailed over my frequent impulses to abandon the enterprise. To Shirley Hill Smith, who labored long but cheerfully through the many typings of the manuscript. Finally, I want to express my gratefulness and indebtedness to Roger Wakefield especially, but to all of the other inhabitants of the Pleasant River valley as well, who so graciously welcomed me into their neck of the woods and without whose companionship and interest this book could never have been written.

DALE REX COMAN

*Pirate's Cove Cottage*
*Bar Harbor*
*Maine*

"*Who* hears the rippling of the rivers will not utterly despair of anything."

*The Journal of Henry D. Thoreau,
November 30, 1841.*

# PLEASANT RIVER

*The landscape is neither a fortuity nor a permanent fixture created by fiat. It is a stupendous masterpiece sculptured from rock by blasting heat and icy cold, cut by the wind, molded by rain, and adorned with life. It is an unfinished masterpiece. The elements, having labored at it for millions of years, anticipate uninterrupted toil for millions more to come. It is the greatest of all privileges to behold their creation and to watch them at their work. Go out and look.*

1

## Introducing the Pleasant

**Why** should a man write a whole book about a river, a small river scarcely deserving the name and noticed casually, if at all, by those who pass over it on their way to somewhere else? I am not sure that I can clearly explain why but feel it incumbent upon me to try, if only as an excuse for intimating that it should be worth a body's time to read the book that has been written.

I am a fly-fisherman. This accounts for my first having visited the Pleasant River, but it turns out that there is relatively little of fishing in the book. I am also a scientist, but this is not the report of a research project. No, I write only as a man who loves the planet on which he lives but who finds the abrasiveness of civilization too much for him unless alleviated, from time to time, by escaping into the out-of-doors. Why do I choose the Pleasant River?

The Pleasant is nearby, an hour's drive from our summer cottage. It is comparatively unspoiled and unpopulated—and I relish solitude. I have come to know the people in its valley and to like them, so there is congenial company when I wish it. These are facts but they do not tell the whole story.

A river makes a deeper impression on me, excites my imagination into more varied and entrancing adventures than does, say, a pond or lake. It has more of mystery about it than has the land-locked water. Wherever you come upon a river, you see it only passing by. Having come from somewhere else and going still another place, it has three parts at any point instead of only one, a past, present, and future; also a birth, infancy, youth, maturity, old age, and death; and yet it never really dies for it never ceases borning.

A river unspoiled, and few they have become, harbors a host of living things that know it as their home. Frog and turtle, May fly and skater bug; trout, chub, dace, and other fishes share their fluvial world with mink, beaver, otter, muskrat. Moose wade the quiet backwaters, their aquatic pasture, grazing belly-deep on the succulent pond weed and water lilies. Deer come down at dawn and dusk to drink. The raccoon roams the shore at night in quest of fresh-water mussels and crayfish. The spotted sandpiper teeters on a rock, the kingfisher rattles, the osprey plunges, the wood duck springs. The honeybee gathers water from the moist sandy spit. The dragonfly haunts the shadows for midges and mosquitoes.

The river knows not only the forest, the limpid spring and gurgling rivulet, the farmer's pasture, moose and beaver; it slides beneath the railroad bridge and trembles with the thundering train; it flows under the traffic of the highway, through village and town. It knows the salt marsh and the gull, the crab and snail, and finally it knows the sea.

Meanwhile, the pond sits between its hills and wishes it were a river. Not that I dislike ponds; I love them, but rivers more so.

## Introducing the Pleasant

Ponds are fine companions for contented spirits who feel no urge to roam or for others who, for a day or year, want only static peace with all held still while they calm their own troubled waters. I have used them so.

Perhaps in my declining years, should I attain great age, I might like to live by a pond, reflecting upon my life as the pond reflects the skies that drift over it. Nowadays, however, I am too restless to be so firmly rooted. My moods change too quickly for a pond to mirror them; a river is my kindred spirit, a river of clean water, its valley still clothed with trees and flowers, where the hermit sings at dawn and dusk, the vireo sounds the noon, and the whippoorwill welcomes night. Where I can live the ecstasy of a rapids, the merriment of a riffle, and the somnolence of a pool, there I would sojourn, from the dissipating haze of morning, through the sun-washed day, to the gathering mists of twilight. From such a place, I take much profit, the intangible products of time spent with profligate abandon, and count my fortune in terms of quiet peace, whimsical thoughts, and of priceless intimacy with the miraculous reality of forests and waters.

Before belaboring further my attempts to justify the perpetration of this volume, suppose we take a cursory look at the Pleasant River itself. Then, if in no way beguiled, you might well close the book and turn to more profitable occupations.

Down from the hills, the Pleasant tumbles and glides through its valley. Spruce and fir, pine, larch, oak, and birch blanket the slopes and press close against the alders that overhang the stream. There are many long, slow stretches where the river winds placidly through woods and blueberry barrens; there are but few white-water rapids, roaring falls, swirling pools, and glistening slicks.

It is a quiet valley, populated more by deer than by people, presenting more of forest than of tilled land. Here and there one comes upon a deserted homestead, slowly sagging into oblivion as trees and brush creep in upon it. The occupants of an occasional farm struggle on, striving to wrest a living from the stony fields and pastures; but they live in an atmosphere that foretells inevitable defeat in the changing ways of our civilization. A few of these hardy souls still try to live as did their forebears who had the fortitude to clear away their patches, full of hopes and dreams. But today this way of life conflicts with the laws of the land. Venison can be obtained legally only within the prescribed season, not when the belly craves meat. Salmon may no longer be trapped in nets, except by outwitting the game warden. The killing of a moose is forbidden at any time; its slaughter must be an act of subterfuge and nefarious scheming.

Whereas the grandfather faced the land with courage and a clear conscience, the grandson, if he attempts to live in the same manner, must wrestle with discomfiting guilt. He must teach his sons to be poachers rather than hunters, outlaws rather than honest tillers of the soil. Either this or forsake the land to lose identity in the distant city. The opportunities for steady employment in the valley are extremely few, posing a problem of deep concern to the thoughtful, sincere, and honest people comprising the bulk of the population.

The Village, living largely in the past, nestles close against the Pleasant. It drowses for the most part, seeming always to be just rousing temporarily from a nap or drifting off into one, but seldom fully awake with the bustle of human affairs. There appear to be more old people than young, more unemployed than gainfully occupied. The game warden, station agent, postmaster, and storekeeper are among the dozen people with year-round jobs; but the volume of mail declines, the daily trains have dwindled to two, one up, one down, hauling a handful of freight and no passengers, while the storekeeper, with fewer mouths to feed, soberly contemplates a diminishing trickle of pennies into the

## Introducing the Pleasant

till. Only the game warden witnesses no decline in his activities. Indeed, he may be hard put at times to keep abreast of them.

Were it not for the modest and sporadic pulpwood operations and the unpredictable blueberry harvest, even this kind of

meager subsistence must peter out. The lobstering business falters along precariously, and when there happens to be a catch of sardines this source provides a bit of welcome income, welcome not only for the temporary reimbursements accruing to the housewives who lay aside their brooms and dish towels to go to the canning factory, but even more for the extended federal unemployment compensation for which it qualifies the participants.

It would be difficult to justify the existence of this hamlet upon economic grounds, as it would, indeed, the entire valley. It costs the country money to keep them alive. I suppose the inhabitants would like to see more prosperous times and the introduction of modern industry. Most of them assert that they would, but I wonder. Why is it they linger on, including a fair number of the youngsters who are well aware of the adversities and limited opportunities?

The answer is difficult to state in understandable and reasonable terms; it has to do with peace rather than progress, composure rather than complexity, sky rather than smog, deer instead of dollars, flowers instead of factories, birds instead of buildings.

The answer has to do also with freedom, personal freedom, and independence.

One ponders long on possible solutions to the socio-economic problems presented by this area of our country. It is difficult to believe that these conditions exist in the nineteen sixties within a few hours' drive of thriving communities more typical of the wealthiest nation in the world. A man is torn between wishing for the advent of some stimulus to the economy and a better means of providing for the populace while at the same time fearing that such a turn of events would be catastrophic to the environment he finds so appealing.

I hesitate to acknowledge that the Pleasant River is in the state of Maine. I confess reluctance in revealing this fact, though the truth would out in any event. My reluctance stems not from selfishness but from fear, fear that in even my fumbling efforts to sing its praises I may be helping to sound a tocsin threatening desecration of the peace, disruption of the simple loveliness of the Pleasant River valley, by calling the attention of a few readers to its existence.

A few more visitors, a few more dollars, but the unexpected, the unlikely, could happen. The Village could, albeit miraculously, become prosperous, with smoking chimneys, humming machinery, and an expanding and affluent populace. Money and people would flow in. What would flow out? I would, of course, but I am of little consequence to valley, river, or village. Far more important, to my mind, would be the loss to our land of still another of those rapidly disappearing oases of the quiet way of life. The quiet, rich, unhurried way of life—the robin on her nest in the pear tree by the porch, the bobolink's song from the meadow, the tinkle of a cow bell, the provocative odors of the general store, daisies and buttercups in the fields, the monotonous hum of insects on a lazy summer afternoon—all of those precious sights, sounds, and smells nostalgic of the wonderful world of a New England boyhood.

And so it is I write of the Pleasant—of its trees and flowers, birds, mammals, reptiles, fish, and insects, and of its people, too, but really, I suppose, mostly write of me and of my reactions to

# Introducing the Pleasant

all of these other things; idle thoughts that come unsought and vague wonderings about things both big and small. I have written about nothing of great significance, just about a man roaming a river valley, what he saw and felt and what flights of fancy came to him there. It seems I had but a flimsy excuse for writing a book after all. I still feel as though I must apologize for having done so, but, if there be those who find entertainment in whiling away their time prowling aimlessly along a river and just as aimlessly meandering wherever it is that thoughts may lead them, the undertaking will not have been in vain, though whatever prompted the creation of this book may remain forever unexplained.

It will be my privilege to act as guide. Before embarking on the journey, however, I must confess to being an irresponsible guide. Indeed, I know not even what we quest. It could be a fine silvery salmon, exciting to capture and delicious to eat, but it might well be only the discovery of where the clematis vine re-

flects its blossoms in some remote spruce-shadowed pool, or only an ephemeral thought. Not a profound thought; I should be frightened out of my wits if I should encounter a *profound* thought. It might be, too, that we shall stumble into the haunts of something as rare and elusive as a moment of tranquillity and catch it, unawares, because it cannot ever be caught in traps set for it.

We shall make no pretense of importance to the expedition because it has none. Equally hopeless would it be to convince anyone that your guide is other than a lazy, shiftless man, somewhat ill-suited to the fomenting times in which he lives, always ready to avoid work and irksome problems to slip away to the woods where he can wallow in utter indolence, while the golden hours glide blissfully away into a sea of pleasant memories.

*If,* when queried as to my destination and intent, I answer, "To the Pleasant River, fishing," the questioner is content. It is socially acceptable for a man to go a-fishing. Should I speak more truly and say, "To the Pleasant River, dreaming," the questioner would doubtless be consternated and speedily pass it on to others that I was at last become quite daft. It is not socially acceptable for a man to go a-dreaming. This seems rather strange since surely far more people dream than fish.

2

## From Dawn to Dark

It is my habit to eat breakfast while driving over to the river. This stems, I guess, either from eagerness to get there or from impatience with merely sitting indoors when I can be rolling through the countryside watching dawn arrive. I pull on my clothes in the darkness and glance through the front windows of the cottage at the sky over in the northeast, across Frenchman's Bay, for some hint, however unreliable, as to the weather. The sky should show at least a wan light and maybe even a hint of color. Then I go about making coffee and some sort of breakfast that can be inserted between two slices of bread—a piece of steak, a handful of fried clams, or a squashed codfish cake, for instance.

I set a steaming cup of coffee on the dashboard of the Jeep but begin eating my sandwich only after pulling out of the driveway and gaining the open road. Usually I am munching on the first bite as I dip down into Salisbury Cove past SKIP'S LOBSTERS, ALIVE OR BOILED.

By the time I cross the bridge onto the mainland at Trenton, it is usually light enough to make out the silhouette of the far shore. If it is low tide, the clam flats will be exposed and there will be gulls, cormorants, and great blue herons to note. High tide may offer seals and black ducks. The sun will poke up above the horizon, assuming it is going to show itself at all, about the time I am taking the curves over at Mud Creek or between there and the Sheep Pasture. From there on it is dazzling in my eyes because I am heading right for it all the way to the river.

When one leaves Mount Desert Island and heads north and east, he is soon aware of being truly Down East. The motels, restaurants, and residences thin out and the trickle of tourist traffic that was not siphoned off by the Bluenose Ferry from Bar Harbor to Yarmouth sticks pretty well to Route 1 and keeps going because there is nothing to stop for. Even the casual observer is impressed with the fact that the human population is neither abun-

dant nor well to do. To scratch more than just a living out of this land requires a degree of ingenuity and dogged determination possessed by few. Spruce forests, blueberry barrens, lakes and streams in the valleys, an intricately sinuous shoreline, with little lobstering villages huddling about the inlets, weathered gray farm buildings, many of them deserted and disintegrating—this is way Down East.

The Village was just opening its eyes on my arrival. I stopped by to see Roger Wakefield at his office on the Maine Central.

Roger was tying up a Mackintosh dry fly. The telegraph was clickety-clacketing, sounding very important the way telegraphs always do, but Roger seemed unimpressed and kept winding in the dark-brown saddle hackles. I asked him who was saying what

to whom, and he said the agent at Machias was asking the agent at Ellsworth where Joe White's pig was that was overdue from Massachusetts.

The clickety-clacketing went on. Roger finished off the head of the fly, daubed it with lacquer, let it dry, and then methodically stowed away the vise, feathers, silks, and so on in the box under his desk and, when the telegraph stopped a minute to catch its breath, he turned to his key and rattled off a short splutter, while gazing through the window up the road toward the Blueberry Factory. I asked him what he had said.

"Told them I got the pig here in its crate waiting for Joe to pick him up. Just fed and watered him. Y'see, Joe called this morning and told me to take the pig off here 'cause he was going to be over this way, and it would save him a trip into Machias."

"Well, why didn't you let those other agents know sooner?"

"What's the rush, Doc? The pig ain't complainin'. And anyhow, they were enjoying having something important like that to talk about."

I drove up the west side of the valley, parked the car, and stood on Arty's Bridge for a while, peering into the river below. A large eel came swimming slowly upstream, and I became lost in thought regarding it. What an incredible creature, the common eel! It commences existence as an egg deposited in the depths of the Atlantic southeast of Bermuda. As the egg matures, it slowly rises toward the surface. Thereafter, the tiny eel, colorless, flattened, transparent, with hordes of companions, sets out on the long voyage to the continents. The European and American eels differ in the number of vertebrae in their spines, otherwise they are essentially indistinguishable; but the little European eels all head for Europe and the American eels for our rivers. When they reach the brackish waters of the estuaries, the eels assume their familiar yellowish-brown color and snakelike form. Most of the males probably remain in the bays and river mouths, but the females travel far inland, up the most insignificant of rivulets, even going overland through dewy grass, wriggling into drain pipes, and squirming up the faces of dams, surmounting formidable obstacles to reach the ponds and lakes where they will grow to maturity over a four- or five-year period. Finally, the spawning urge is stimulated by their endocrines, and they journey back down to the estuaries where they are greeted by the waiting males. Together they swim to that one spot in the sea to spawn and die. Why, oh why, and how did it come to be so?

I pulled the canoe off the carrying racks, lowered it into the river, and paddled up to the Alders, Flat Rock, Spring Brook, and above. The pickerelweed is not yet in bloom, nor arrowhead. Iris and yellow pond lilies are at their peak. The water was fairly high from recent rains, but there were few fish in. I had a snooze after lunch during the hot, midday period and loafed away the afternoon, mostly sitting and not thinking about much of anything, except how comfortable it was to be just sitting and not thinking about much of anything except how comfortable I was —both inside and out.

# From Dawn to Dark

Returning to Flat Rock in the early evening, I cooked my supper while watching for a salmon that I sort of hoped I would not see, because then I would have to stop watching and start casting.

The thrushes put on a wonderful serenade—four olive-backs, two hermits, and a robin going full tilt all at once, with a white-throat, a red-eyed vireo, and an olive-sided flycatcher for background—altogether a magnificent symphony.

There was a great hatch of midges, some nearly white, others dark; mosquitoes, too; and dragonflies; and a hatch of small, dark May flies that I was unable to identify in the failing light. Other pale May flies were mating over the stream while chubs and salmon parr gorged themselves on the insects.

It was a lovely evening, the silently sliding river darkened by towering spruces and larches, their shadows and reflections stretching all the way across the stream, and the murky darkness of the water broken only by ripples around rocks or by silvery circles where a parr or chub took a May fly. Meanwhile, the thrush serenade poured forth in full ecstatic loveliness. A varying hare came hopping down to the water's edge to feed, flopping its long ears, and now and then scratching itself.

A blue jay screamed, a red squirrel chattered, and at once all other sounds ceased. I, too, tensed and cocked an ear. Something was stirring—man, wildcat, fox, what? Something had prompted jay and squirrel to sound the alarm, and every creature paused, pricked its ears, alert, and waited. Then I heard footsteps and the brush of spruce boughs against a moving form.

Young Bruce Worcester stepped out of the woods and sat on the bank with me. He had been weeding beans all day. He had

his rod with him but did not fish. We just sat and talked and watched the river until he left to keep a date with a salmon he hoped would show up at the Alders at dusk.

As not uncommonly happens when I sit alone by the river in the forest, looking at the sky, the flowing water, the rocks, and the mantle of living things that covers the ground, I became acutely aware of the awesomeness of endless time and the incomprehensibility of infinite space. At such times I feel pitifully ephemeral and inconsequential in this huge sweep of things; and yet I am permitted to witness it, in a brief and wondering glance, and to flounder about in the somewhat frightening reality of my own unexplainable existence. Even so, I would far rather possess some feeble conception of the significance and direction of the whole than total cognizance of my own evanescent and minuscule sojourn.

Thoughts come unsought; you cannot set out to capture one.

# From Dawn to Dark

Good or bad, happy or sad, frivolous or serious, they are suddenly there, without warning. Surely, they arrive only to the mind prepared to receive them; but how is such a preparation to be made when the thought itself is unknown until already at hand? Once there, it can be consciously and voluntarily (?) developed and expanded, turned, twisted, and embellished; but often it is not easily abandoned until replaced by another. Thoughts, then, may be difficult to come by and no easier gotten rid of. You cannot shake them loose by giving them to someone else, though sharing the burden of them with a kindred spirit may lighten the load. So many thoughts, though, are too vague to permit of precise expression; these one must carry on his own shoulders and bear to live with, alone.

From far up on the ridge there suddenly came a startling whoop—not so much a war whoop as a shout of exultation that

echoed back and forth between the hills and finally died away, leaving a silence that seemed even deeper than before. A stranger would wonder, I thought, at how to account for this wild outburst but, to those of us who knew it well, it could only be—Roger.

The first time I had heard it he and I were fishing together, only a short distance apart; and I had asked what prompted the sudden yell.

"Can't help it, Doc. It's so good to be here, alive, and along the river and everything that it just comes out that way, all at once. Can't hold it in, that's all."

In a few minutes I heard him coming down the trail. We sat together in the twilight watching the river and sky and the varied activity of living things, while the thrushes fell silent and a whippoorwill called.

Roger musingly observed that the Pleasant River had, since childhood, seemed to him a mysterious thing, "... running to the sea its whole life, but always right here." I thought of that other river that I have always treasured as *pleasant,* despite its moments of anguish and sorrow, that also seems destined to flow for a lifetime without really getting anywhere. Just before dark, several salmon moved up into the quick water, and we cast until we could no longer see our flies but failed to rise a fish.

We parted, Roger to climb back up the trail to his car, I to slide downriver in the canoe to the Bridge. I drove home through a beautiful, star-sprinkled night.

***Dawn*** *and dusk are my favorite hours. I love their shadows, long, cool, deep mysterious shadows. If there be such, I am a shadow rather than a sun worshiper. The creation of shadows I consider to be one of the sun's major activities, perhaps no less important to the living world than its blazing noonday heat, and far more lovely. It is from the halflight that enchanting thoughts and wonderment spring; brilliant illumination reveals only facts.*

3

# A Visit to the Narraguagus and Speculations about Circles and Straight Lines

**If** one waits long enough, some gorgeous days arrive Down East. Rarest of all is a "typical Maine day," when skies are crisply blue and white, the air cool and balmy, the landscape glowing with foliage and blossoms, and the waters reflecting all.

Today dawned in the most grandiose and spectacular manner. The entire eastern sky shimmered orange and pink and the smooth bay reflected and enhanced the glory of it from shore to shore. Sky and water were distinguishable only by the violet band of spruces that separated them; a truly magnificent display. It seemed a pity that so few residents and summer visitors were abroad at four-thirty in the morning when the show was at its peak.

I decided to stop off at the Narraguagus River, at Cherryfield, having heard that there were now salmon in the Cable Pool and that nearly two hundred had been passed up through the fishway of the new dam at Stillwater Pool. I fished at the Cable, but upon taking the river's temperature found it was running a fever of seventy-four degrees Fahrenheit and was not surprised that no salmon came to my flies.

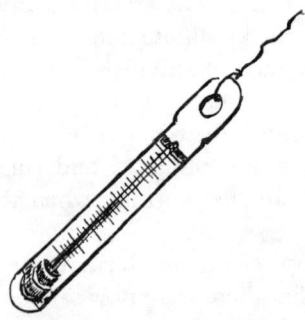

Since I was on the 'Guagus, I thought I might as well spend the rest of the morning there. I used to fish this river often a few

# A Visit to the Narraguagus and Speculations

years back, before my love affair with the Pleasant had blossomed, but, since the ice-control dam had been installed, I had not explored the river above. I slid the canoe into the river and paddled upstream through the long deadwater that was created by the dam. Where the West Branch comes in, I found that the confluence of the two streams now forms a sprawling body of water more akin to a lake than a river.

I pushed on. The shores of the river are here crowded with small willows and the speckled alder. There is a great variety of trees behind this border, fine stands of birch, spruce, and aspen, with elms, oaks, ash, red maple, white pine, wild cherry, an occasional hornbean., larch, locust, and cedar scattered among them.

Spatterdock, arrowhead, water lily, and pickerelweed grow in the quiet shallow coves. Cedar waxwings; purple finches; robins; hermit and olive-backed thrushes; barn, tree, bank, and cliff swallows; chimney swifts; yellow warblers; red-eyed vireos; olive-sided flycatchers; chickadees; red-breasted nuthatches; ravens; crows; a great blue heron; two little green herons; kingfishers; hummingbirds; an osprey; a sparrow hawk; and several black ducks were among the birds I noted. I saw a pair of rough-winged swallows and believe this may constitute a northernmost record in the breeding season.

Two adult black ducks were in their postnuptial moult and therefore flightless. They flapped and skittered ahead of the canoe and finally darted into the dense growth at the stream's edge. Two others of their kind were young birds, two-thirds grown, also flight-

less. They peeped apprehensively at my approach, and one of them dove and next appeared behind me. Many people are unaware that black and other "puddle ducks" can dive and swim under water pretty well, though not nearly so skillfully as their "diving duck" cousins.

I paddled upstream for about three miles in all, coming at last to the foot of the quickwater I had been expecting. There I left the canoe and waded up through the rapids. Brigades of white birches marched down the steep bank and teetered at the brink. Most of the water was too shallow to hold salmon. I inspected each pool carefully but found no fish. At the head of the fast water, I came upon the entrance of a spring brooklet and hoped for a salmon or trout where its cold water spilled into the river but caught only a ten-inch smallmouthed black bass and a big chub.

I returned downstream, convinced that no salmon were now in this stretch. I came upon the footprints of a man and the remains of a fire that I reckoned to be about ten days old; that is, since the last big rise of water but before the recent little shower. I wondered who he was and what he was doing here but, of course, would never know.

On the way back to the dam at Stillwater, the long paddle was aided somewhat by the sluggish downstream flow and by a gentle though fitful breeze. Three crows flew by, arguing with

# A Visit to the Narraguagus and Speculations

each other. I saw several muskrats, two beavers, the protruded head of a big snapping turtle, and many small schools of shiners and dace. Beaver dams blocked all of the rivulets as they entered the river, creating flowages behind that sent the backed-up water

into the aspen groves. Branches of aspen, their bark chiseled by the beavers, were floating here and there. The aspen is the staff of life to the beaver. Deer tracks traced every sandspit, bucks, does, and the tiny hoofprints of fawns; this is good deer country. I saw a well-used otter slide on a steep clay bank. The black ducks repeated their evasive tactics on my return, where I found them in the same coves they had occupied on the upstream journey.

The river winds and twists in this section, sometimes almost imperceptibly, at other times sharply changing direction. I would be headed straight toward a rocky mountaintop for a while, only to notice a moment later that it was now way off to my right or left, or out of sight entirely. Then it would loom up unexpectedly almost behind me, only to reappear next before me, so meandering a course does the stream follow.

I arrived at Stillwater Dam with that pleasant well-exercised-muscles feeling and ate a huge lunch before pulling the canoe out, lashing it on the racks, and heading on east. I would now go over to the Pleasant.

On the drive, I reflected upon the country I had just explored. "Beautiful" and "unspoiled" were the adjectives that flitted into my mind. This implies that where man treads he spoils and makes ugly; despite the fact that he designates the areas he has appropriated as "improved." Pursuance of this thought always leads me into a sea of conflicting facts, unsortable, difficult of evaluation, and coming to no definitive and satisfactory answers. I am soon hopelessly bogged down in a morass and cannot ever drag myself out of the mire onto dry land again with the quarry I was chasing.

Conservation I am forced to view sadly as but a delaying action, while continuing my contributions to conservation organizations and wishing with all my heart that I could entertain happier prospects for the future. The problem strikes me as hopeless for several reasons. Perhaps most painful is recognition of the fact that so very few people are other than indifferent to the naural environment and most are content only when the pristine has been sullied with hot-dog stands, motels, television sets, water skiis, outboard motors, dance halls, and moving-picture theaters. The most relentless and seemingly unavoidable threat to the preservation of our land, however, is posed by the increasing population and its demands upon our resources for power, roads, homes, industries, wood, and so on. A burgeoning economy and exploding population are inimical to preservation of the natural terrain, and it seems unlikely, short of a horrendous cataclysm, that the population, in the foreseeable future, will dwindle or the economy become static. This all comes down at last to an appraisal of values, but who is to do the appraising? The majority, I suppose; and the majority do not even know the natural, much less regard it as a priceless possession that once lost is lost forever.

I like to see man harvesting and utilizing the bounty of Nature—different woods for various purposes; tilling the soil for crops; raising animals for wool, leather, milk, meat, eggs, and so on; water; oil; coal; and gases. This reliance upon natural resources emphasizes man's oneness with other living things—the beaver in his lodge, with aspen branches stored away, the man in his house, with stocked pantry. If only man were not so crassly destructive and edacious about it. Each generation lives as though all is for their own gluttonous consumption, giving little heed to those who are to follow. Also, whereas pains are taken to keep the deer population in ecological balance, man does essentially nothing to curb the frightening increase of his own kind. It is safe to say, and has been said, that the most important and terrifying single problem confronting man today is the rate at which his numbers are growing; but one sees only occasional references to it and no concerted serious action is taken to avert the certain catastrophe that impends.

I am always somewhat frustrated when following my thoughts in these directions. Indeed, the question arises, for how long a journey should one ever embark upon so frail a craft as a thought? So many such ships quickly come to grief on the shoals of confusion, are destroyed in battles with other thoughts, or become stuck upon the sandbars of futility. My own thoughts are prone to have difficulty keeping to their proper course and, buffeted by the winds of doubt, becalmed by lack of power, or buried in a fog of indecision, are lost to wander forever hopelessly through uncharted seas.

Hunting and fishing would seem inimical to the conservation concept, but there are arguments to support the opposite conclusion. For example, such national organizations as Ducks Unlimited and Trout Unlimited are composed of sportsmen who devote strenuous effort toward increasing the numbers of ducks and trout.

Fly-fishing is one sport wherein the entire essence of the pursuit and capture of the quarry can be enjoyed without detrimental effect. That is, the fish can be released unharmed after the fray is over. More and more anglers are adopting this simple expedient for perpetuating and improving their favorite avocation. I have found great satisfaction over the past ten years in releasing almost all of the trout and many of the salmon captured. Unfortunately, a similar procedure cannot be applied at the conclusion of a successful shot at bird or mammal.

I find myself torn between my love of hunting and those compassionate viewpoints that have crept into my way of thinking. Long ago, I laid away my rifles. In recent years, I have thoroughly disgusted my setter dog, Huckleberry, by allowing the shotguns to gleam untouched in their cabinet. I do not know for certain that this noble conduct will persist. I can easily conceive of situations wherein I might well succumb to the temptations of going afield again. Thus can a man be torn between his strong primitive drives as a predator and his earnest wishes to attain to a loftier state. As you see, that little ship of thought we set sail upon has carried us far out into an ocean of uncertainty and may never be able to find its way into port again. Ah me.

When I arrived at the Pleasant, I tramped up to the Spring Brook. On the way, I startled a doe in a small clearing. She stood there a moment wondering if I was worth the sacrifice of another bite of clover, decided I was, and sauntered resignedly into the spruces.

I cast for a few minutes desultorily. I had but little inclination to fish for some reason I did not bother to investigate. I lost three of my best flies in the alders. A stream fisherman who does not know the speckled alder is certainly not an observant person. This shrub is always reaching out its greedy fingers to grasp the angler's fly and, once caught, the grip is exasperatingly tenacious. If a man could recover the artificial flies clinging to New England's alder branches, he would need trunks to hold them.

A goldfinch, blithely singing at his work, looped a scalloped border for a cloud. A green frog sat like a stoic in the shallows, waiting patiently for some flying insect to come near enough to jump at.

On my return to Flat Rock, I dozed away several hours, hypnotizing myself by watching the stream's glide. Water is such beautiful stuff, whether flowing as a river, floating as a cloud, or rolling as the sea; wherever it is, it is beautiful, due to the fact that light both penetrates it and is reflected by it. Water fascinates everyone, especially when in motion. The child is entranced with

# A Visit to the Narraguagus and Speculations

the gushing faucet or garden hose, the streaming gutter, and the advance and retreat of wavelets along the beach. Adults gaze spellbound at the surge of the ocean, the cresting waves and pounding surf, or the gentle glide of a river. A happily tumbling brook is a thing to elevate the spirits, to put the world aright.

I noticed the developing seeds on a burr reed, and it set off a train of thought about the cycles of natural phenomena. Every race in every land remarks the cycles of the seasons. I believe the American Indian depicted Nature as a circle, indicating not only the recurrence of spring, summer, fall, and winter in endless sequence but the lives of men as beginning and ending with childhood, and the moon and sun as circular also. But, does this cyclic pattern pertain over the longer, broader scope of things? It would seem to me not. History does not repeat itself, however much current events may simulate preceding ones. I believe dinosaurs existed for longer than man has as yet and have been extinct for longer than man has lived. However it be, dinosaurs have never returned and almost certainly never will. In this sense, species, even genera, appear on the vine of life as the blossom on that clematis over there. The blossom comes into existence, performs its functions, withers, and dies, while the vine goes on growing. That blossom will never reappear. Man is not now what he was when he emerged as a bud on the primate vine, nor will he ever return to that former state. Life, then, is not so much a circle as a continuous line that started in the unknowable past and is destined to progress into an unforeseeable future until, at last, in the end it will cease, on this particular planet at least. Evolution did not stop upon its discovery; it continues today as it always has.

This planet, too. Unless the universe as a whole follows some cycle so large as to be unrecognizable, it also seems to conform to a straight line rather than to a circle, despite the "curved" nature ascribed to space by the physicists and astronomers. This earth, having come into being as a new aggregation of materials heretofore incorporated in some other body or bodies, has a destined lifetime, predictable by man or not. When the day comes that it is destroyed, no doubt its substance will be utilized in the formation of some other structure or structures; but the planet Earth will not exist again. It is like the clematis blossom that in decay will participate in the production of some other expression of matter, living or inanimate.

# A Visit to the Narraguagus and Speculations

I guess we like to think of cycles because they are tight and comfortable little circles that cannot wander off into frightening unknowns; but since fear is reputedly due only to ignorance, why should we cling to an unsupportable concept for security? Why not live in the constant expectation of always knowing more?

The obvious cycles of Nature are fascinating and one can draw from them all sorts of intriguing analogies to man, but are such speculations profitable? As soon as I begin to pry into the matter and attempt to push this cyclic concept to anything beyond the appearance of spring after winter, of seeds reproducing their own kind of plant, of chipmunks begetting chipmunks, the cycles evaporate or break open and unfold to become straight lines, beginning who knows where or how, stretching out behind and ahead, intersecting and branching from each other to form an intricate maze, but, having come from somewhere, they are obviously headed elsewhere, and that does not describe a circle. A circle goes round and round upon itself, having neither beginning nor end. So much for cycles; I end up with straight lines.

A chill in the air aroused me, and I could scarcely believe that the day was fast drawing to a close. Where had it gone? It had seemingly dissipated with the morning mists, but I did not try to account for the hours I had squandered. A pair of wood ducks came flying upstream, flared widely upon seeing me, then at once swung back over the river as they continued up it.

I cooked my supper in the twilight, lighting a small fire and throwing some green grass on it so as to produce a smudge to force away the mosquitoes, now coming out of their shady retreats. A bullfrog uttered sonorous pronouncements from across the river. I did not leave until night fell, so had a long tramp through the dark forest to the car.

On the drive home, I reviewed the day and decided it had, after all, been one of those truly lovely ones when from dawn to dark one little adventure had followed another, and the sun had shone down, and the breezes had wafted over all, and when, at day's end, the muscles ached comfortably with that wonderful feeling of having been used as they were intended. Though tired, it was the gratifying fatigue of good health and exercise in an enchanting environment. Such days are so few in a lifetime, so inexpressibly wonderful, and one drifts off to sleep with a happy mind replete with delightful memories. To have taken a salmon would have been too much. The day was complete as it was.

"*And* lastly, I am to borrow so much of your promised patience, as to tell you that the Trout or Salmon, being in season, have at their first taking out of the water, which continues during life, their bodies adorned, the one with such red spots, and the other with such black or blackish spots, as give them such an addition of natural beauty as, I think, was never given to any woman by the artificial paint or patches in which they so much pride themselves in this age."

Izaak Walton,
**THE COMPLEAT ANGLER**

4

# The New Canoe

As I pulled her off the carrying racks, I wondered what name I should call her by. This was to be her maiden voyage, and I was eager to test her character, appraise her potentialities.

Mona, Charity, and I had driven over to Old Town the previous day to pick her up at the factory. She had been built to order: no keel, extra half-ribs, very light planking, and a thin coat of hard enamel instead of the heavier lead-containing paint. The ladies had avowed she was pretty, quickly adding that she was, in fact, altogether too lovely and fragile a thing to submit to the savage attack of rock-filled rivers. I agreed she was beautiful but insisted she must have some character as well. She had a mission in life. Hers not to dally amongst preening swans on a placid lily pond; hers to run the rapids, the foaming white waters, the knife-edged boulders, despite her tender frailty.

I slid her into the river where she rode pert and high, like a teal. She responded quickly to the paddle and obviously was happy to be in her proper element. We negotiated the first set of rapids. She shuddered at the first painful contact with a jagged rock but regained composure and settled down to business with the proper spirit and determination. I guessed we would get along together and maybe someday she would develop that dauntless imperturbability that her predecessors had had. Time would tell.

We glided through a long stretch of slow water. It was one of those cool wet mornings, gray and dripping, when you cannot be sure whether the air is filled with fog or fine rain. Thoreau used the word "drisk" to describe it, and who am I to propose a better term? The river was high; the alders' feet were wet.

Beneath the alders, myriads of expanding ringlets indicated where accumulating drops had finally become so heavy as to fall into the river whenever a feeble breeze stirred the twigs and leaves. A gloomy raven flew over, uttering its customary complaints about the world. A muskrat towed a widening triangle of ripples behind him as he crossed the river. It was serene and still in the dark spruce forest. At a distance a fire-charred stump appeared like a bear; a rock simulated a strange duck or a hunched-up beaver; the scraggly branch of a dead spruce looked for all the world like the antlers of a deer in velvet. Such little illusions key you up only to let you down again, but they do keep you alert.

Red splashes of cardinal flowers, white streaks of arrowhead

# The New Canoe

blossoms, and blue spikes of pickerelweed painted a patriotic border to the stream and in it, too, where the dark water harbored their wavering reflections. It was a good day to be off alone on the river, cool enough to make exercise pleasurable, not so wet as to be uncomfortable. An entirely suitable day for basking in silence and solitude.

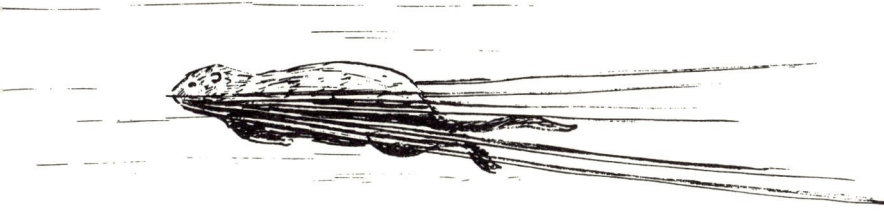

The canoe nestled her nose in a bed of pickerelweed, and I stepped out onto a shingle of fine sand. I stood there, watching and waiting for anything that chose to entertain me. It turned out to be a kingfisher that flashed by on a seriously important mission, and he felt it necessary to interrupt the peace and quiet with a raucous rasping rattle as he disappeared around a bend.

A large dragonfly, *Libellula*, the kind I had learned to call a "ten-spot" when a boy, attracted my attention. She was laying eggs. Holding her body vertically on vibrating wings, she jabbed her rear end down through the water into the mud at the stream's edge. She did this swiftly half a dozen times in one place, then darted along a few feet and repeated the performance. The depositing movement was fast, forcible, deliberate, and accompanied by a great buzzing of the wings. I recalled reading that the larvae of these insects—truly fearsome miniature dragons—prey upon recently hatched salmon before the salmon have forsaken the redds.

I jointed my rod and mechanically threaded leader and line through the guides and tied on an odd-looking brown-and-white dry fly that knew neither name nor kin. It was one of those that hatch out unpredictably on my fly-tying bench of a winter's evening as a result of some great inspiration. I selected it at random because that was the casual and contented way I happened to feel about things today. I had not given a thought to salmon all morning.

On the opposite side of the stream a wee brooklet dribbled into the river just above a sizeable boulder, the tip of which barely protruded above the slowly swirling water. Had I been dwelling intently upon salmon, I would have climbed a nearby tree and searched the pool before bothering to cast. As it was, I did not care much whether a salmon was there or not.

I waded out into casting position, inadvertently sending a series of waves across the pool before awakening to the fact that I really was salmon fishing after all and perhaps had better buckle down to it and stop this absent-minded daydreaming. It did look enticingly fishy, that sluggishly eddying water, and I gathered my straying wits to cast the fly into the slot between brook and boulder, then watched it as it came drifting prettily downstream, seeming to float on a film of air above the water, rather than actually on it, so lightly and gaily it rode.

The water bulged, a salmon took. I set the hook and was jarred wide awake. This was a delightful battle from start to finish

# The New Canoe

—dazzling leaps, somersaults and cartwheels, lightning dashes, surging runs, frantic moments with weeds and snags, heart-sinking periods of sulking and bull-dogging, and finally a silvery salmon lying on a bed of sphagnum in the canoe.

With due solemnity, I removed a scale and a drop of blood from the salmon to place them on the bow of the little craft and announced to the chipmunks and chickadees that henceforth her name would be *Princess Salmo Salar*.

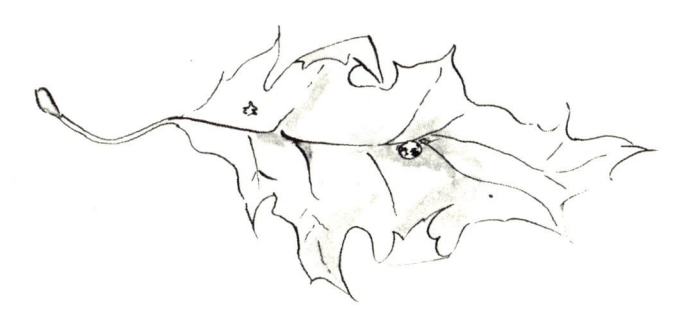

As I knelt by a spring to quench my thirst, I tipped over a brown oak leaf that was serving as container for a raindrop. The dislodged droplet fell on a piece of shale and ran down it, leaving some of itself in its own path, and then spilled into the spring and lost visible identity as its molecules intermingled with those other millions of molecules comprising the water of the spring. And yet, I thought, the individual atoms of these molecules will persist forever as entities on the planet. They may travel the trickling brook into the river and thence to the sea, or become incorporated in a lily pad, the fin of a chub, or the tail of a muskrat—or they may now be residing in the lobe of my left ear, since I drank as I thought. In any event, they will not be lost because when lily pad, chub, muskrat, or I am through with them, they will pass on to continue their endless wanderings through the centuries, having come into being whence and how?

This oneness of life is appealing and exciting to me. Indeed the unity includes the inanimate as well, when looked upon at this atomic level. And so it is with you and me and with the trees and rocks and sky and sea—everything is merely a temporary aggregation of restless atoms, none of them permanently located and each one varying in its degree of permanence in any one place, but eventually traveling on, either when excreted, evaporated, eroded, or when the entity of the organism ceases to exist as such —dying, we call it—when it is released at last through the disintegration of its host.

Thus is immortality the way of atoms, and thus are we, composed of atoms, immortal in our component parts and thus, too, do we participate fractionally in the reincarnation of other living forms throughout the ages. A growing baby or a poplar sapling does not represent the creation of any new material but merely a reassortment of the original and permanent supply. I find it entrancing to realize that I am composed of the identical cosmic dust of which our planet was first formed and which has been in the rocks, the sea, the clouds, in dinosaurs, toadstools, and in my cave-dwelling ancestors, and that I will pass it on through eternity.

There is, I repeat, something appealing about this oneness to me, and I enjoy immersing myself in reveries concerning the possible histories and futures of my constituent atoms, fruitless though such ruminations be. In any case, it gives one an undeni-

# The New Canoe

able sense of *belonging*—an intimate relationship with every facet, past, present, and future, of the entire universe.

We had a good day, the *Princess* and I. It was nearly dark before we turned downstream. Thoreau's drisk had become a hard, wind-whipped rain. We lingered beneath a tall pine to listen to the eerie white sound of wind through its top. It was a good sound with which to end a day.

*Hya, Harry. Say, where's Bob?*
*Bob? He's down to the diner tellin' about that salmon he caught.*
*Oh? Bob got one, did he? Where did he catch it?*
*Right there, where you're fishin'.*
*What time?*
*'Bout seven-thirty.*
*What fly was he using?*
*Number four Cossaboom.*
*Big fish?*
*Fourteen pounds two ounces.*
*Fresh run?*
*Ayuh. Bright as a dollar.*
*I'd like to see it. Where is it?*
*Dunno—by* now—*jest where it* would *be.*
*What do you mean by that?*
*Well, 'twas seven years ago come September he caught it.*

5

## Of Turtles and Teenagers

**On** the way over to the Village, a doe with twin fawns crossed the road. I passed several handsome patches of fireweed in the clearings. The fields were ablaze with happily integrated communities of daisy, hawkweed, and buttercup.

I learned from Roger that outlaws have been netting quite a few salmon these nights. At over a dollar a pound, it is too much of a temptation for some to resist, even though they have to accept the possibility of Don Higgins catching them at it; the fine is a stiff one. The Pleasant, running as it does through mile after mile of forest, most of it not readily accessible, presents a staggering problem to patrol effectively; and the netters work together, posting lookouts and so on.

I paddled upstream, having launched the canoe at the end of the tote road on the west side, and soon located two fish, one of which sunk a White Wulff on the first drift and thereafter declined all offers. The other salmon took a tremendous leap and then fell back into a long piece of deadwater, leaving a big wake.

I decided to reverse my direction and drifted downstream beyond the clay bank to where Little River enters, and there I spotted a salmon and got one rise out of it without fastening.

The golden day dissolved in a crash of thunder and a torrent of rain. I barely had time to pull the rain jacket out of the back pocket of my fishing vest and to struggle into it before the shower went sweeping off into the forest, mumbling and grumbling over the hills. The shimmering, dripping leaves and grass blades were

# Of Turtles and Teenagers

bathed in warm sunlight again, and the sweet musty odor of drenched forest filled the air, until a fresh dry breeze from the southwest wafted it away.

At noon, I tethered the canoe to an alder and drove into the Village for a hamburger at Rosie's. Several of the town's teenagers were there, sucking soda pop through straws but talking mostly—the young males extending themselves to deliver wisecracks, while pretending to ignore the twittering, giggling females for whose ears the remarks were obviously intended. Other than for the rural vernacular and bucolic manners, they could be teenagers anywhere, the same basic motivations guiding each generation through age-old traditional patterns of conduct, whether adorned and modified by culture and sophistication or uncouth, rustic, and simple. They were happy in any case and were still going strong when I left. If only they could afford to be as free with coins as with time and verbiage, Rosie would prosper famously.

I chatted with Pat Oliver, sitting on the porch bench at the Store. Pat drifted down here from Canada and stayed. He said he had some loggers back in the woods cutting pulpwood. Pat blames the poor fishing on the killing of black salmon in the early spring.

On the way back up the valley, I passed the teenagers who had left Rosie's and were walking up the dusty road, the girls ahead, still giggling and now and then glancing quickly back to make sure the boys were following along twenty yards behind, scuffling in mock battles, hurling stones, and every so often sending forth great guffaws over their incomparable witticisms.

I returned by canoe to cast over that salmon. A little spit of sand juts from the bank at the mouth of the branch. A movement near it caught my eye and a closer look revealed a snapping

turtle with a carapace about a foot and a half in diameter. I recalled seeing a dead alewife some yards away and went to fetch it. This activity sent the turtle into the deep water. I placed the fish on the sand, sat down, and waited. Before long the turtle cau-

## Of Turtles and Teenagers

tiously returned, spending long periods staring suspiciously. Gradually, it advanced and at last seized the herring and pulled it under the water.

It took the turtle one hour and ten minutes to eat the fish, which was a good-sized one, grasping it with hooked beak then clumsily pushing against it with its claws until a piece was torn free. The reptile would then lie still for several minutes before making a sudden gulp, sending the chunk of flesh on its way to the stomach. The whole process was completed while the turtle was submerged. The entire fish was consumed except for the head. Whether this snapping turtle had an aversion to fish heads or whether its hunger was satiated I do not know. At last the turtle gave me a long scrutiny with its cold little eyes and then cumbersomely turned and, with outstretched neck, swam slowly off into the dark depths while I eased my cramped and aching muscles.

Snapping turtles have an air of the ancient about them; they hark back through aeons of time to the geologic age of the evolutionary dominance of their kind. The ancestors of this recently made acquaintance were probing the ooze of river beds for countless centuries before my earliest progenitors, the primitive mammals, had made their timorous appearance on the planet. Since the evidence appears irrefutable that mammals derived from reptiles, I must view this cold-blooded patriarch of the Pleasant as my granddaddy. I find this kinship pleasing, even though the turtle is blissfully ignorant of our relationship, and I have no way of communicating the information to him.

Antiquity seems to lurk close beneath the rough, drab shell and behind the cold, fixed, emotionless stare of reptilian eyes and in the ponderous movements as the sluggish beast swims down into the deeps—where, in the sediment and rotting vegetation of bygone years, it slowly lives out its days unaware that the Mesozoic has ended and knowing naught of the energy of atoms nor the taste of Winstons.

A rifle shot rang out and reverberated between the hills. I was pretty sure whose eye had lined up the sights and on what, but there are times and circumstances when it is more discrete to ignore what one perceives through his sense organs than to exercise his duty as a conscientious citizen in upholding the laws of the land. It is not that I condone the breaking of game and fish laws; but laws are so inflexible and human motivations, needs, and circumstances so various that my judgment becomes hazy and befogged in trying to distinguish right from wrong; justice from mercilessly imposed hardship; or so I happen to feel about it sometimes when in the valley of the Pleasant.

In the evening I cooked supper, still having failed to rise the salmon, though I had tried hard to do so. At eight-thirty, in the gathering dusk, the salmon rolled again, and I started casting in the fading light while mist gathered in the valley. Just at dark the salmon took, and I fastened, only to break on a snag minutes later. I went over my boots and fell down while groping around in the darkness.

I paddled back up the river through the mist that shut out the stars. It was so dark I had trouble finding my launching site but finally made it, pulled the canoe ashore, changed my dripping clothes, and was soon on my way home. A fine big wildcat crossed the road near Tunk Lake.

So ended another day without a fish, but it was interesting, what with teenagers, turtles, and such.

**Hi**, Doc.

Hya, Joe.

Been up in the back country with your Jeep lately, Doc?

Day 'fore yesterday.

Figger I c'd git through t'the mouth o' the Mopang with my car, Doc?

Nope. Too wet and soft, Joe.

Good. I feel better.

How come?

Well, Doc, y'see if you'd told me I could git in there I'd undertake t'go and o'course it'd be hard work makin' it in 'cause you know, it always is, and then I'd hafta fish all day and afterwards, when night come, I'd have that long tough drive back out 'cross the barrens when I was all tuckered, and I'd come home hungry, wet, and wore out. This way, s'long 's I can't git in there it saves me all that hellish hard trip for nawthin'—'cause o'course they ain't no fish up there this time o' year anyhow. Don't y'see?

Of course, perfectly clear.

S'long, Doc.

Bye, Joe.

## 6

## June Twenty-second

I awakened at four-thirty to the sound of rain on the cottage roof. Huckleberry, the setter, aware of the weather, did not ask to go out, just opened one eye, sighed, hunched himself into a tighter curl, and went back to sleep. The bay and sky were but one element, all water, completely masking the distant mountains. I decided to go to the river anyway.

The rain fell steadily, but I launched the canoe below Arty's Bridge and pushed upstream to the deadwater stretch near the clay bank. A fine Canada lily with ten blossoms appeared to be enjoying the rain. I saw a swirl ahead, close under the alders, so went ashore and waded out on the clay shelf. The first drift of a dry fly produced a bulge, and on the next I was into the fish but slipped on the clay and sat down, waist deep. I could barely move on standing up because of the weight of water in my boots, so I released all tension on the line in order to calm the frantic salmon while I spilled out some of the river I had collected. Then I coaxed the fish into a downstream run where there was more water to maneuver in and fewer obstacles. It was a grand contest and the prize a bright female of about fourteen pounds.

A northeast wind sprang up. I was soon shivering, so I paddled back to the car, undressed, wrung out my clothes, and put on another set. It is my custom to carry extra clothes, tied up in a bundle and stored in the Jeep for just such emergencies, not infrequent to those who play with rivers.

For no reason at all and despite the drizzling weather, I decided a walk was in order and soon found myself descending the

## June Twenty-second

trail through the woods into Flat Rock. I came upon a patch of forest floor carpeted with bluets, their winsome faces peering up from the dark background of fallen spruce needles and beds of moss. These dainty things always bring into my mind a fleeting vision of white-haired, sweet old ladies clad in dresses speckled with little pink and blue flowers. Maybe I saw bluets on someone's gown in childhood, or is the association with females dependent upon another name for them—Quaker ladies? Still another name is Innocence, and indeed they express it.

Nearby was a sedate society of twinflowers, also one of my favorites and the first encountered this year, so I must lie down on the soggy ground to smell them. Twinflower may have been the pink florets on those ladies' dresses. This small plant is distinguished by having been chosen by the great naturalist, Linnaeus, as his namesake—*Linnaea borealis.*

Bluets and twinflower. They seem such fragile things, with slender stems barely able to support their tiny flowers, yet here they grow in the northern forest, blooming, whether seen or not, and producing their almost microscopic seeds to fall into this huge earth, towered over by pine and spruce. Though the environment appears suitable for only the ruggedest forms of life, the delicate and minute thrive in the embrace of soil, air, water, and sunshine because Nature is so. Does not the lichen on the rock yield its grain of sand to the shores of the sea? And what manufactures this rich humus out of dead leaves and twigs, huge stumps, and even whole windfallen trees but bacteria? Plants so small as to be invisible to the naked eye. That tremendous white pine, reaching far up into the sky, even above the rim of the valley, is dependent for its survival upon these multitudes of microbes that prepare its food for it. So much are the great and strong dependent upon the small and weak, and so even twinflower and bluets live to the benefit of other things, though their beauty alone is adequate justification for their existence.

As I look about me in this forest, I see scarcely a square inch devoid of a life-covering of some sort. Like a huge blanket, life-covering lies over everything, assuming an endless variety of form and texture, of color and size; but what I see is all life, the whole vast skein, interwoven, interdependent, stationary or moving, furred, feathered, scaled, flowered, or whatever; what I see is that wondrous mysterious thing we call life, and, fragmented and separate though its expressions may appear, life is but one great unity, a unity that includes bluets and twinflowers as well as you and me.

I drove down to the pool by the Town Hall and watched it for half an hour, but no fish moved. A broad-winged hawk flapped and soared across the valley harassed by a belligerent kingbird. Leland Grant came along and stopped to chat for a few minutes. He was lugging a suitcase containing samples of shoes that he carries around from door to door in the valley taking orders. He lives alone in the weathered farmhouse on the east side of the valley. He said he was too old to farm the land now; told me to feel free to cross his place to the river, but the tote road has grown up so with brush and trees it is rough going even with the Jeep.

I drove up the east side of the valley. Dan Look was nailing siding on his new garage. I stopped in at Norris Pineo's. Norris has an aversion to nonresidents of Maine but lets me use his road, if you can call it that, into the river. He and his cats were eating in the kitchen. None of them said much.

I decided to walk in to the river, though the rain continued. It was a long wet tramp through the dripping woods. I followed the ridge and finally came to the river opposite the bulldozed road on the west side and fished from there down to the mouth of Little River. I stopped on the way to admire a handsome growth of

## June Twenty-second

spotted jewelweed, or touch-me-not. I found a place where a gill net had been set across the river and was quite sure who was responsible for it but decided I would forget its discovery.

There is something satisfying about viewing one's inconsistencies as quite reasonable and acceptable and with a clear and happy conscience. It *is* possible to *need* a salmon.

It suddenly seemed strangely lonely on the river—far, far away from all the rest of the world. I guess it was the monotony of the rain, the dull dreary colors, and the silence—no bird songs —just the soft whisper of rain on the grass and leaves and the pattering of it on my rainshirt and hat.

I sat under a spruce tree a long time trying to keep my pipe lit and wondering how come I was here while everyone else was some other place, probably warm and dry, and talking to each other about all sorts of important things and laughing at jokes, maybe, and saying how bad the weather is and looking through the window at it, waiting for it to change.

I was soon relishing each delicious twinge of my melancholic mood, soaking up the sweet sadness of solitude while the seat of my pants soaked up moisture from the soggy turf. The poignancy of such moments is always enhanced by wistful recollections of a host of similar episodes in which I was wont to indulge as a boy. And then a red squirrel discovered me and shattered the silence, as well as the delightful agony, with his chattering fuss. Red squirrels are hams, always over-playing. I heaved a stick at him to give him something worth-while jabbering about.

Realizing that it was getting late, I took only a few more casts before starting the journey back. It was now dark and no let-up in the rain. I drove on up the east side, crossed over the Bridge to the west, and went up the hill past Orrin Worcester's place where

warm yellow light glowed comfortably from the windows of the old farmhouse. On down to the Village—more lights from more windows. There were no people on the street, but shadowy figures moved around in the Store. One of them was Pat Oliver and another was Dan Ingersoll and, I guess, Morris Tibbets, but I could not be sure, and Ken and Sim, of course, waiting on folks.

I pulled onto the highway and headed for home, then saw a light in Delia's and realized I was hungry, so picked up a lobster roll to eat as I drove, washing it down with the coffee that was left in the thermos.

I stopped in at Charlie Shoppe's Fly Shop in Franklin. Charlie's wife was there. She had just come from the doctor's where she had had a fishhook removed from her left leg. Her son had hooked her on the first cast with a Rat-faced McDougal. I offered condolences.

Three deer stood in the road outside of Trenton, and a wood-

## June Twenty-second

cock slammed into the windshield near the Wagon Wheel; I collected it for its feathers.

Warm lights again, twinkling from the cottage this time, where Mona, Charity, Michael, and Huckleberry were waiting for me. So endeth a rainy day in June.

*S'pose Bion could make me a part t'hold this contraption together?*
*Ayuh. Bion ain't here right now—be back in a minute.*
*I guess Bion can make it all right. He gin'rally can make most anythin' s'long's it ain't important—like a livin'.*
*Figgered he could. What d'ya think it'll be worth?*
*Nawthin'—but 'twon't cost much more'n that.*
*Sounds reasonable. I'll wait.*

7

## Alewives and Daisies, Trout and Harebells

**Leaving** the cottage before dawn, I watched the sun gild the bay as it poked up from behind Schoodic Mountain. Parties of daisies and buttercups tripped merrily through the fields. I stopped by at Roger's office. Don Higgins, the game warden, and Charlie Joy were there. Charlie was reminiscing about a salmon with which he had had an encounter a year ago; Charlie reminisces in elaborate and colorful detail. Later he left for the Machias.

Roger and Don were writing up the regulations governing the taking of alewives from the river. These herring belong to the township. The residents may vote at Town Meeting to sell out the netting rights if they wish or they may decide instead to allow each resident to take a specified number each day during the season, using a dip net. No one else is permitted to catch them. The alewives are sometimes smoked for eating purposes but are more often used for lobster bait or cat food.

I once tried to trace down the origin of the word "alewife" and came upon two possibilities. One was that it was derived from

79

an American Indian word, *aloofe;* the other was that it was applied in a jocular vein because of the resemblance of the spawn-filled fish to a corpulent ale-drinking wife.

The train had gone through so Roger pulled the big lever on the wall to drop the signal that tells the train behind that it is safe to go through—but there never is any train behind, because this single train is the only one that runs the track between Ellsworth and the Canadian border.

I put the canoe in at the Bridge and went downstream to fish the pool above Wash Rips and then returned upstream, fishing all the pools and slicks as far as Spring Brook. Iris and water lilies are in full bloom. I saw no sign of a salmon, so ate my lunch and took a nap, then paddled slowly back to Arty's Bridge and took the canoe out. A demure cardinal flower, attended by a hummingbird, gazed enraptured at its image in the stream. I felt like a Peeping Tom caught spying upon a lady before her mirror.

Richard Bailey came by driving a tractor with mower attached. He was cutting grass and decapitating daisies along the roadside. I could not see that it helped anything—except Bailey,

### Alewives and Daisies, Trout and Harebells

who was glad to have a paying job with the Highway Department. I suppose we have enough daisies around here to sacrifice a few so that Bailey can buy meat and bread for his wife and children. We did not discuss the matter; talked about important things like the weather and the scarcity of fish.

I returned to Roger's just as he was closing up for the day. After he had locked the door to his office and we were standing outside wondering what to do, Roger said, "Doc, I feel like having a mess of trout. There aren't any salmon in anyway. Let's drive up to Montegail Pond." So we went into the Village and picked up a loaf of bread, some corn meal, butter, salt and pepper, and then drove up across the barrens to the pond. Nobody was there; we had it all to ourselves. A pensive wild rose stood in a clearing longing for company.

We each picked a spot where a spring sent in a trickle of cold water and began casting our flies. We soon had a dozen brook trout of eight- and ten-inch length. We cooked these and ate looking out over the water and seldom speaking.

It was quiet on the pond save for a pair of loons, their lonely cries echoing back and forth. The sky was overcast, soft gray.

Trout were rising here and there. A great blue heron slanted down for the far shore, going frogging probably. A few birds were singing; whitethroats, of course, a chickadee, two olive-backs, and a purple finch. I discovered several harebells growing near a rocky outcropping.

We left in the twilight and drove across the rolling barrens as the sun slipped behind the spruces. The warm golden highlights of evening are supported by strong shadows. Shadows are true substance, highlights only superficial, gaudy embellishments. When, at midday, all is evenly lighted, colors are bleached out, vapid, unprovocative; without the dark side, the bright is not glorious.

On the drive back, Roger was telling me something of the history of the Pleasant River Valley. The settlement was formally established in 1863, having emerged from the status of a Plantation under the administration of Massachusetts. (The acceptance of Maine as an independent state of the Union did not occur until 1820.) In the early days, the inhabitants of the community were engaged in shipbuilding and there were several lumber mills along the river. Canadian ships came to purchase salt hay from the coastal marshes. The first doctor arrived from London, England, in 1799, a man named Haskell, having been preceded by the first clergyman, Reverend Joshua Young, a year earlier. For one year the community could boast of its own lawyer, Thomas Goodhue, who dwelt there from 1807 to 1808. Evidently his services were not so essential as to gain him a livelihood.

The greatest period of activity along the Pleasant appears to have been about 1850, and the population hit its peak of 698 persons in 1890. Since 1910, the population has steadily declined to the present figure of 423. Roger is one of the three Selectmen who administer the affairs of the Township. Joe Pineo's lumber mill is the only one still in operation.

I enjoyed this interlude in the salmon season. All in all, it was one of those nothing-much-happened days that are soul satisfying, in a lazy comfortable sort of way. A June day. Simple, unhurried, peaceful—when my other world, the university and the city, seemed ever so far away and not very important.

I feel sorry for the weekend fishermen or those who have only a day now and then to be on the streams. They miss so much. It takes quite a spell of fishing to become truly immersed in the surroundings and to wear off the need to catch a fish and, as a consequence, not have time to catch anything else—like the bliss of solitude, the odor of clethra, the song of a thrush, or the silhouette of a spruce against the sky. It takes a good while to step out of one world into the other—completely, that is, and if it is not completely it is not at all really—it is stepping into the one, but pulling the other along with you, on rubber bands that stretch so far and then snap you back before you have actually become free.

***Ca'm*** *down, Ken! What ya stompin' up a storm about?*
**Broke my leader.**
*Let's see it. Hell, that's nothin'. Here, let me tie on another tippet for ya.*
*Oh never mind, Bill. 'Tain't the leader so much. Lost my fly, too.*
*Good one?*
*I got better. 'Tain't really the fly so much neither. Busted the tip of my rod.*
*That's too bad, Ken. I'm sorry.*
*Oh, I got a extry tip. Guess 'tain't* that *bad, Bill.*
*Well, then, what in blazes* are *ya fussin' about, Ken?*
*Cuz I jest now lost the biggest damn salmon I ever see, ya stupid fool,* and fer gawd's sake quit remindin' me of it!

# 8

# In July

**Rain** and fog with an easterly blowing. I like these gray, dripping days. The misty atmosphere makes even the most familiar objects seem enchantingly, mysteriously different. An old house that holds neither charm nor interest in sunlight now glooms through the wet gray haze enshrouded with sullen, eerie mystery. So different do things appear that you can pretend to be visiting some other planet. Boulders and trees assume fantastic shapes, belying their true nature. A native larch might be an unknown species towering into the vapors of some unearthly cloudland. The appeal of a larch lies in its ragged ungainliness anyway; each tree always seems to have one arm that is too long to manage gracefully. Fog also distorts the size of things. A sparrow hawk perched on a power line looks to be as large as a gyrfalcon. Thus does fog transform the commonplace, lending it the entrancement of strange environs heretofore unvisited.

Wild roses are now blooming in conspicuous profusion. Isolated blossoms dot the roadside and great clumps of them glow in every field and clearing. The majority of these are *Rosa nitida,* the northeastern rose, but I have also found *R. humilis,* the pasture rose, and *R. virginiana,* the dwarf wild rose. These single-flowered, invariably pink, wild roses vary chiefly in the size of their blossoms, the thorniness of their stems, and the character of their leaves. In addition, there are the roses that still bloom on ancient bushes that hide the crumbling foundations of houses built in colonial times and the errant progeny of these old plants may be come upon most anywhere. Their blossoms contain many petals, and they may be white, pink, or deep red. Steeplebush, or

hardhack, and meadowsweet, the two common spireas of this area, are in flower, the tall pink and white plumes poking up from rank foliage on tough stems. Daisies, buttercups, the hawkweeds, evening primrose, vetch, purple and white clover sprinkle the fields with brilliant contrasting colors. The early goldenrod, *Solidago juncea,* is now showing a tinge of gold where the plants are situated in sunnier places.

Summer—all the warm mellifluous richness of it—the luxuriance of knee-high timothy with its caterpillarlike seed clusters, the lustrous greens of healthy trees, the grand display of flowers, young purple finches and black-capped chickadees with gaping bills and quivering wings, the crops burgeoning from the brown earth, tomato and potato, corn and bean. The sun blazes down at midday;

# In July

the dawn and dusk are cool with long probing fingers of shadow from which come the songs of thrush and whippoorwill. Opulence and grandeur, bathed in rain, heated by the sun, and cooled in the dewy darkness of July's magical nights.

I dropped in at Roger's office to see how he was doing and to pick up any new river gossip he might have to offer. Somehow everything finds its way to Roger. He is sort of a one-man information bureau for the Pleasant River valley.

Don Higgins was there. He had a problem. A summer resident owned a dog of which he was very fond; but the dog chased deer, and **Don** warned the owner that he, as game warden, would have to kill it if this went on. The problem was how to train the dog not to chase deer.

Don suddenly had an inspiration. He picked up the phone and called George ———, a notorious outlaw who owns a pack of assorted hounds that he trains *to* drive deer; he ought to know the answer. The brief conversation went like this:

"George, this is Higgins. Got a problem. How do you stop a dog from chasin' a deer?"

"Hell, Warden, that ain't no problem. Shoot the deer!"

I found Allan Gay at the Alders with his brother, Ernest. Allan had moved a salmon several times, and the fish rolled at his fly again while I watched. He said he had had three or four fish rising at dawn, but none would take. The Gays soon had to return to their fruit-and-produce business over at Jonesboro. I told them

I would not disturb their fish so that they could come back after work in the evening and try them again.

When I watch other men fishing, I often wonder what goes on in their minds while casting their flies. Most appear to be concentrating with all they have on fishing and fish, which, I suppose, should not really be surprising. Others evidently enjoy even more the social aspects of group fishing, the chatter, banter, and fraternizing. Very few convey any indication of an aliveness to their environment, other than the pool in which they cast their fly. Surely, however, there must be other fishermen as easily diverted by a tree, bird, or beaver as I. Do they also *dream* for who knows how long and only occasionally awaken with a start to find themselves fishing? This makes me wonder if it is fishing I like about fishing. I do so little of it while doing it. Perhaps it is better not to pursue the thought further; I might be led to give up my favorite avocation. Still, I wish I knew what others think about when fishing.

I finally located three salmon, and two hours later one of them took a dry fly, but the ensuing fray was short lived. The leader fouled a snag and snapped.

Wearied of casting, I ate lunch while sitting on the bank of the river. Refreshed and with interest rekindled, I bestirred myself to climb a tree and was reassured that two salmon remained in the pool, lying deep. Nothing I did stimulated their interest throughout the afternoon.

Having had enough of profitless fly-casting, I sat on a rock for a long time, daydreaming. The thought came from somewhere that the boulder on which I sat was but a fragment of mountain, dislodged and deposited here thousands of years ago by a mass of moving ice. Before that it was a few bucketfuls of the molten matter that had cooled and congealed into a planet, as it drifted through space until caught and held captive in the invisible grasp of a star's gravitational fingers. It had been an integral part of this corner of the universe for ages of time and would, in all probability, continue its existence for millenniums after my momentary appearance and disappearance. And yet, I thought, I have the consummate effrontery to sit upon this wondrous bit of celestial stuff as if it were of no more significance than a second-hand footstool.

In the evening, I cooked an early supper, or, rather, heated up a bowl of clam chowder that I had brought along in a jar, embedded in ice cubes in the little carrier I use for that purpose.

I am extremely fond of both beef stew and clam chowder; that is, so long as each is built in the way that *I* build them—which would require several pages of meticulously imprecise directions, since one needs to be carefully casual and cautiously reckless in such undertakings. I would like to be able to construct either for a meal at riverside, but there seem to be unsurmountable obstacles. When I have fabricated one or the other of these meals at the cottage, I always tote along a quart or so on the next day's trip to the river, the luscious product having been improved even beyond its original delectability by having slept overnight in the refrigerator. Then, I have only to heat it—and relish it. But I am apprehensive about *building* a stew or chowder by the stream unless, of course, I am encamped there for several days or longer because a certain bulkiness to the thing is, to my mind, mandatory. To construct one having only the dimensions of a single helping, even for a ravenously hungry man, strikes me as a rash and dangerous venture. An edifice consisting of a potato, an onion, a carrot, a handful of peas, a few hunks of beef, a sprinkle of salt and pepper, and a couple cups of water, even Pleasant River water, would bear the same relationship to a genuine stew as a log cabin to a mansion. I may prefer log cabins to live in, but I want my stews to be mansions. It is the same with a clam chowder, but more so. Whereas I may entertain a suspicion of doubt about the stew and may, even, on some day that I feel especially devil-may-care, attempt to produce a miniature facsimile of one at the river's edge, I am quite positive that a chowder, to suit me that is, could not be fashioned successfully from a potato, an onion, a few clams, a cup of powdered milk, a smidgin of salt pork, and a dash of pepper. *That* would be like building only one wall of the cabin. I just could not abide in it.

Henry Patterson came down to chat and watch me fish. He was born and raised here in the valley; learned to swim in the same hole where his sons and daughters are learning. He described how he lives and provides for his family in the valley of the Pleasant, obtaining meat, fish, fowl, and berries. He raises his own vegetables, and his wife freezes or cans them. He and the boys trap beaver, otter, and muskrats for furs to sell. During the hunting season, he acts as guide and picks up some money that way. Sometimes he takes a temporary job working on the roads, and he and his family pick blueberries during the harvest. He also raises some sheep, keeps a cow for milk, slaughters a couple calves and a pig, which, supplemented with deer meat, fish, and birds, sees them through the year. It is gratifying to realize that the frontiersman spirit and independence are yet alive in our land.

In the gathering darkness, I paddled down to the Bridge. Ernest Gay was there. He had seen my car and knew that I would be coming back alone, so he had waited to help me pull the canoe up the steep bank and load it onto the racks; a fine gesture, I thought.

I left the Bridge at nine-thirty for a long, hard, fog-shrouded, nerve-wracking drive to the cottage. I barely missed a careless doe while going over Catherine Mountain. I stopped for a talk with a raccoon at Fox Pond but found him remarkably noncommittal on even the most controversial subjects. He gave the impression that he was nettled at being interrupted on his way to the shore and his mind was doubtless dwelling on the fresh-water mussels he was after rather than upon my erudite conversation.

I later missed a meditating porcupine by inches and, over by Mud Run, had to wait while a skunk ambled disdainfully across the road. Skunks and porcupines are among the few creatures that can afford to be utterly independent. They are free to ignore convention and to express blithely their own uninhibited personalities. They have had little need to learn to fear, but the penalty they pay for fearlessness is ignorance. Not many animals are so stupid, and I can say this with considerable assurance, having known them on intimate terms for years. Despite the fact that they are not remarkable for sagacity, they are extremely interesting animals nevertheless. I am fond of them—and a little envious, too.

Things happened today but did not add up to much in the way of tangible profits. I saw some salmon. I was fastened to one for a few electrifying moments. I met and talked with good friends. I enjoyed it, even the hazardous drive home. In retrospect, I guess you cannot ask much more of a day.

*Where ya headin'?*
*Fishin'.*
*Better not. Storm's makin' up.*
*Yup.*
*Ain't any fish in the river anyway, is they?*
*Nope.*
*Then why ya goin' fishin'?*
*Never said ketchin'. Said fishin.'*
*Oughta wait 'til tamorra. The rain'll raise the river tonight and maybe bring up some fish from the bay.*
*Could be.*
*Then why don't ya wait 'til tamorra?*
*Cuz.*
*Cuz why?*
*Cuz I might not* wanta *go fishin' tamorra.* Today I do *wanta. Nothin'* else *don't make no odds.*

# 9

## When Nothing Much Happens

**There** are those times when salmon play no part in the proceedings of a day that is ostensibly spent in their pursuit. The minor adventures experienced while the hours drift by are woven into the skein of one's existence without relation to fish, except that their quest has brought the individual into the environment in which the events occur. There are apt to be many such days on the Pleasant—more than of those others when salmon play the dominant role. The fishless days are seldom wasted, and, whereas nothing much may happen, they still add up as satisfactory and may linger on in memory after more exciting days have been forgotten. Since such days do occur with more frequency than the others, they merit consideration, and I feel compelled to depict one, if for no other reason than to present a balanced picture of salmon angling on the Pleasant River.

It is well along in August. Summer is slipping fast away. One becomes conscious of it on the drive over in the early morning. Here and there a red maple blazes in scarlet splendor or perhaps only a single branch of an otherwise dull green tree. I have never had the reason for this precociousness explained to me—why the pigments of oxidation should form so early in one branch or in a single tree while all the adjacent branches and trees continue to wear their summer foliage.

The grasses are turning brown. Buttercups, daisies, and hawkweed no longer sparkle in the fields. Instead, goldenrod and asters predominate, while evening primrose lingers on. Saint Johnswort and the great mullein add to the abundance of yellow gold in the landscape. Clusters of black-eyed Susans brazenly stare unabashed at each other.

Shore birds are already in migration, and the swallows are gathering in flocks on the power lines. Mourning doves still spring up from the road as I drive along, and the pair of bobolinks that nested in the hayfield are tarrying there yet, but the robins are forming loose and restless groups and one senses that autumn is gently pushing summer off the stage.

There is an early autumnal activity among the human inhabitants of the river valley also. It is blueberry harvest time. Trucks loaded with crates are rumbling down from the hills toward the distant cities, while out on the barrens men, women, boys, and girls, native and Canadian Indians, are stringing lines to mark out the picking lanes, scooping up the berries in their rakes, pouring

# When Nothing Much Happens

the fruits into winnowing machines, packing the berries into baskets, the baskets into crates, and the crates into waiting trucks, and thence to the "factories" for further winnowing, inspecting, freezing, canning, or packaging.

There is a bustle around the big gray building of the Pleasant River Canning Company at the edge of the Village. Trucks are coming in with berries, men are loading and unloading crates, housewives from miles around are sitting in rows inspecting the berries as they travel by on an endless belt. The berries in this plant are cooked and canned. Labels are not put on until the wholesaler purchases them, when he attaches his own brand name. The business details are handled by the Company, which functions as a cooperative.

For the transportation of workers, equipment, and berries, every available piece of rolling stock in the valley is pressed into service, including the yellow school buses, which carry the housewives to and from the factory and their homes. Indeed, if the harvest is delayed because of unseasonable weather, the opening of school must be postponed until it is completed. The economic factor necessarily takes precedence over all other concerns, including education, if only in order that the schools can be maintained.

To assure production of berries and to keep in check the growth of other plants, sections of the barrens are burned periodically, usually every second year. Hence, you overhear particular areas referred to as "Luther Sawyer's new burn", or "Tabbit's old burn", and so on.

Whereas a few days before you could gaze out over mile upon mile of empty landscape, now there are people everywhere. Don Higgins says, "Doc, don't kick any old roll of tarpaper you come across; chances are there's an Indian inside it. They're in and under every shack and woodpile in the country." While I am pulling the canoe off the racks and gathering my fishing gear, the voices of the berrypickers float down into the valley from high up on the rolling barrens, lending a bucolic atmosphere to a land that lives in silence most of the year.

Roger's honeybees are working the goldenrod along the river bank, gathering their last precious loads of nectar against the long flightless, flowerless, winter months when, in the cold darkness of the hives, the clusters will shrink tight against the honey-packed combs.

I push upstream to the slick by the Alders, joint my rod, select a fly, and am about to start casting when a pair of mink interrupt me. I do not understand their antics. It appears to be play. One comes slithering up onto a log, shakes off a scintillating shower of droplets, and runs along the log to its outer end. The other mink does the same and chases the first off into the river, and the whole performance is repeated. Then a variation takes place; the first mink runs back toward the pursuing one and becomes pursuer instead of pursued, and the merry-go-round turns in the opposite direction. All of this strenuous exercise seems to accomplish nothing, unless to a mink's heart it brings joy and happiness. Suddenly, both mink vanish—a marsh hawk comes soaring along as silent as its shadow, now lifting up to hover a moment, now drifting off on a long glide, its sharp eyes searching, scanning, hunting.

Several monarch butterflies flit by. Strange that so fragile a creature should yield to the urge of migration with all its attendant hazards. So few of them must survive. These are feedings as they go, sipping the nectar of the late summer flowers. One alights upon an aster nearby, and I walk cautiously over for a closer look. I can see its long siphon tongue, downward bent, poking into the blossom. I have noticed that cabbage butterflies and sulfur-yellows are often scattered amongst migrating flocks of monarchs. Do these species also migrate? This is one of those things I should have traced down in the literature long ago, but I always forget to do so.

There are so many of these things—unanswered questions

arising from casual observations—that I have little hope of ever catching up with them. Even so, my store of utterly worthless knowledge is so vast as to threaten the exclusion of almost anything of practical value. I have no trouble discoursing for one hour or a dozen on the life of the honeybee, the history of fly-fishing, the fauna and flora of the countryside, the surface characteristics of cancer cells, or any one of a thousand other equally unprofitable subjects; but damned if I have ever yet figured out my income tax correctly, and I am completely ignorant of how the stock market works and how to use public transportation in a big city. I confess, also, to unqualified stupidity about modern music and the undoubtedly important statements on my insurance policies and deeds to properties.

Actually, it is only in the woods and along the rivers or sailing on the bay or ocean that I feel secure and self-confident. Back in the city, I have to place my security and welfare in the hands of others, and the result is that I am too dependent upon too many people to feel comfortable about it. Even when exploring a new river in my canoe or threading my way through an unknown forest, I know where I am and, if not where I am going, at least how to return. I can only hope that someone else knows where a bus or a subway train is taking me. I also feel confortable, relaxed, and safe back in the woods. Nothing there will harm me, unless my own carelessness results in an accident. Out on the highway, I am a vulnerable target for every reckless or drunken driver I meet. Thirty thousand people are killed on the highways each year. How many die in the woods? Most of the few who do should not have been there in the first place, or they were killed by that ubiquitous enemy, their fellow man.

It is time for a cup of coffee and a smoke on my pipe. While enjoying these little pleasures, I sit on a flat rock and gaze at the river. Dragonflies are cruising up and down along the banks, hunting midges and mosquitoes in the shade of the alders. I hear several ruffed grouse, clucking and fluttering about beyond the nearby pines and spruces. There are some ancient apple trees over there, and I can visualize the handsome birds at their feast. Great clusters of wild cherries hang from trees close by. Waxwings and robins are feeding on them. A bald eagle sails high across the sky, spinning huge circles as it rides the invisible thermals. Most of the time, the bird appears as a solid dark object but, every now and then, the sunlight flashes on its white head and tail. Last year a pair of these birds nested here in the valley. They failed to raise young, however, and this year I have seen only this single adult. It has been around all summer—looking lonely up there wheeling about in the big sky or sitting on its favorite perch, the skeleton of a dead white pine.

I pole the canoe through a shallow rapids and then paddle on up the river through a long run of slow water. A small mammal is swimming across the stream, having just left its western bank. At first glance, I think of a muskrat but dismiss this at once—it is too small. It is not long enough for a mink nor does it swim like one. I bend my back to the paddle and spurt ahead to intercept the animal. It is a chipmunk! This is the first time I have ever seen a chipmunk swimming. He rides high in the water, paddles his feet with considerable commotion, but moves ahead rather slowly. He comes right up to the canoe, and I pull ahead to let him pass. On he goes to the shore, scrambles out, shakes himself, and darts off ino the spruces. Why did he make this formidable journey? Was he being chased by a fox or weasel? Or did he just decide to satisfy his curiosity about what lay on the other side of the big water—a Christopher Columbus among chipmunks?

# When Nothing Much Happens 103

I poke along upstream, flushing a pair of black ducks as I round a bend. Two woodpeckers are working over a spruce tree.

They are neither downies nor hairies. I shove the canoe ahead quietly and finally obtain an unobstructed view at a short distance; they are arctic three-toed woodpeckers, the first of their kind I have found in this area. This sort of discovery is satisfying. You feel good about it, as though you had accomplished something worth-while, though just what would be difficult to explain to most people. Come to think about it, it is not very clear to me either.

Giddy troops of arrowhead are wading in the shallows, while haughty ranks of pickerelweed disdainfully ignore them.

I wade out to mid-thigh depth to cast over a wide swirling pool at the mouth of a spring brook. There might well be a salmon or two lying here. Having had no response, I wade back to shore, take off the fishing vest, and climb a tree—a tall larch, or hackmatack. Once started, it is comparatively easy to go on and on until far up in the topmost branches. From this vantage point, I can scan the bottom of the pool with no difficulty. There is not a fish in it. However, the view over the treetops is beautiful, and it is fun to have this eagle's look at the winding river below.

It is well past noon. I paddle across the river and climb onto the steep bank, taking the knapsack with me into a cool shady place from which I can look out on the river. The spring brook gurgles happily nearby. I rummage through the pack to find sandwich and coffee and, with my back comfortably nestled against the bole of an oak, eat my lunch. Nothing of any consequence occurs. A well-burdened bush of wild raspberries provides dessert.

I have a smoke and then start on up the river, not with any particular destination in mind, but because there is no point in going back downstream, and the only other way to go is up. That is one nice thing about a river. You have only two choices to consider, up or down, whereas on a lake or pond the possibilities are so many that it can be quite disturbing if you just feel like going but have no precise destination in mind.

I have not paddled on the sun-drenched river for long before the combination of lunch, heat, and exercise result in heavy sleepiness. I tether the canoe to the overhanging limb of a white birch, allowing the craft to swing in the slow current under the leafy shade while I stretch out on the bottom, with knapsack for pillow, and soon drift off to sleep.

I awaken to the spluttering call of a northern yellowthroat.

# When Nothing Much Happens

An inchworm dangles on a strand of gossamer that I trace to a twig high above. Through how many ages have inchworms been performing these gymnastics and to what avail?

The afternoon is well along. The sun is far enough over in the west that its searing heat has diminished somewhat while a light breeze has sprung up from the southwest. I paddle a few hundred yards upstream and leave the canoe on a rocky islet halfway up a shallow rapids. A dour and ponderous boulder, soberly studying its wrinkled visage in the river, seems anything but pleased with what it sees.

There is just a remote possibility that a small pool along the east bank, above a plunging pitch, could contain a salmon. In any event, a walk in the woods is attractive so I work my way through the alders into the forest.

Deer tracks are everywhere. A red squirrel chatters annoyance at my intrusion. Here is a pile of dissected spruce cones on an old stump where the squirrel has been feeding. A junco and several whitethroats flit over the forest floor. A deer path affords easy walking and facilitates maneuvering the fishing rod through the trunks and branches. In a soft, moist, sandy depression I come upon the fresh tracks of a bear and notice that the right forefoot shows only four toes and leaves me wondering what happened to the fifth. I sneak ahead quickly in hopes of catching sight of the bear in the next clearing but this enterprise is doomed to failure, if only by a second; I get a glimpse of waving branches as the bear is swallowed up in the seclusion of the forest.

The pool at the head of the pitch is empty save for a sick-looking lamprey. Lampreys are abundant in the river. Earlier in the season, hordes of them have migrated onto the spawning beds from the sea. Every so often I find a scar on a salmon where a lamprey has clung as a parasite. Jim Fletcher, the biologist, says that they do smooth out and clean up the river bottom for salmon redd-building and, thereby, may be rendering a service to the salmon to make up for their more despicable traits.

The lamprey was once highly esteemed as food and still may be so used in some parts of the world. I have seen the phrase "jugged lampreys" in this connection, but I have no idea of what the "jugging" consists. I have read that their flesh is not easily digested and that Henry I of England died as a result of overindulgence in lampreys, his favorite dish. They arouse no appetite in me, but I am fond of the common eel, oysters and clams, lobsters and crabs, none of which look palatable except through familiarity, so I might enjoy lampreys. After all, if they were fit for the King, who am I to condemn them?

Many people would prefer that our rivers were devoid of lampreys; but, when one tampers with the natural state of things, unforeseen calamities too frequently ensue so it is better not to meddle. Lampreys and salmon have coexisted for centuries, and the tragic reduction in the latter species has occurred through the depredations of man, not lampreys.

I tramp on up to the mouth of a fair-sized brook that enters the river from the east. Salmon do enter this stream, but whether to spawn or just to bask in its cooler flow I do not know. It is quite shallow now, and I doubt if there are any salmon in it. From this point, however, there is a nice view up the river. This is all fast water, tumbling over rocks, big and little, with here and there bright patches of sandy shoals. Spruce and pine tower from the banks, trying their best to touch the sky. They provide just the right kind of background for the white water. I would like to paint this stretch, but it is a long way to lug easel, canvas, and paintbox.

On the way back, I take a slightly different course and happen upon a clearing that is actually blue with blueberries. That black bear knows all about it because his signs are all over the place. I see where he has lain on his belly while sweeping the dead-ripe berries into his maw. I do just about the same thing until cloyed with their sweetness.

A large patch of New England asters are nodding their deep-blue heads at each other, and beyond them evening primroses, goldenrod, and several late wild roses provide a colorful backdrop. Somehow the *concept* of a flower is even more beautiful than the blossom itself, the *idea* of life being no less exquisite than its reality.

By the time I arrive at the canoe, the hour is at hand to slip down the river to that slick by the alders, where I started to cast in the morning—a mile and a half or even farther away—but my progress now is steady and easy, with the current's help, so it is not long before I wedge the canoe between two conveniently arranged rocks and step out into the shallows at the head of the slick and seek that flat stone to wait and to watch—for a salmon, I hope. Meanwhile, I pull out the one-burner stove, a pot, a pan, a potato, and a piece of meat and cook supper.

I can look down to the Bridge from here. The swallows are putting on a display of aerial acrobatics that affords delightful entertainment. Great numbers of them are sitting on the wires. Others are whirling and skimming about over the water, every so often plunging their breasts into it and shattering its mirror to fragments that resolve into expanding circles of ripples. Dozens at a time are doing this, each bird seeming possessed by a frenzy to outdo the others in its reckless display of bravery and skill. I find myself caught up in their excitement. There are tree swallows, barn swallows, and a few cliff swallows in the flock—and it is a gay party they are having. Soon they will be facing the more sober and dangerous business of flying to the southern limits of this continent and still on into South America and far enough down it to be in summer again. Cedar waxwings are fluttering back and forth, making like fly-catchers, and a catbird is flitting through the alders doing the same. Overhead, several nighthawks cut through the air in swift erratic flight, uttering harsh nasal calls.

The sun drops behind the spruces, and a chill sweeps into the valley. Orrin Worcester's truck, filled to the brim and overflowing with his four young sons and three daughters, together with their friends, had rattled across the Bridge, up the road, and over the fields to the swimming hole, and now it comes rattling back again—the children laughing, shouting, whistling. They wave gaily to me as they cross the Bridge. They have all been picking berries out on the sun-scorched barrens since early morning. The swim in the river has put them in boisterous fettle and has no doubt stimulated tremendous appetites. The truck rolls on out of sight on its way to the rambling farmhouse at the top of the hill, on the west side of the valley.

A hermit thrush sings. The song of the hermit is probably the most beautiful bird music in America. Quite likely the hermit thinks so, too; he never seems to tire of it.

I stay until dark, without having seen a salmon move. I have spared myself the useless procedure of casting a fly over empty water. It is now time to paddle down below the Bridge, where I left the car this morning. On the way, a big round moon, wondrously bright, pokes up above the hills and looks down into the

### When Nothing Much Happens

valley of the Pleasant. Three woodcock dart across the river from the northeast—migrants or natives?

I pull the canoe up the bank and secure it to the carrying racks; pull off my boots and slide my feet into the old slippers; stow away rod, reel, and other paraphernalia; and then relax from these small labors to bask in the beauty of the moon-flooded valley. The river is a ribbon of silver against the velvety blackness of the spruces. A whippoorwill calls, and the day when nothing much happened is done.

*"**Man** was meant for summer, and summer for man—
not summer of the desert and dusty sands, but summer
with running water in the cool murmur of the hills.
And what better excuse is there for being there than a
fly-rod in one's hand?"*

> *Roderick Haig-Brown,*
> Fisherman's Summer
> *(William Morrow & Company, 1959)*

# 10

## Of a Day in Summer

**This** was a humid, sultry morning that promised to be hot in the river valley. On the drive over, I slowly became aware that my mind was amusing itself by dwelling on the current explorations of space; then it went on wandering while I, half consciously, saw the rocks, trees, dirt, and flowers flitting past the window as I drove. It occurred to me that the original mass of which our planet was composed had, during its millions of years of existence, accumulated additional small increments of material from those meteoric bodies that had collided with it. That is, it had actually gained a modicum of mass since it had lost nothing, save perhaps some wandering molecules from its outer atmosphere.

But now, it suddenly struck me, man, the enigmatic biped, can hurl hunks of this planetary substance out into the far reaches of space, where these tiny pieces of Earth will revolve in new orbits around the star that is our sun, lost to us forever as homeless waifs, derelict in the infinite, never to return to the mass in which they had cosily rested since Earth was formed. Man thus tears out chunks of the planetary ship he rides and casts them overboard to see what becomes of them and, by his marvelous ingenuity, compels these bits of flotsam on the seas of space to inform him as to what they discover out there. Meanwhile, he expends most of his talents and industry in perfecting machines exquisitely designed for the sole purpose of exterminating himself.

I was unable to arrive at any satisfactory correlations or conclusions that would reasonably embrace these two astonishing and bewildering activities that, on the one hand, seemed to justify unstinted faith and boundless admiration for this amazingly clever two-legged mammal but, on the other hand, relegated one's spirits and hope to a bottomless pit of sickening despair. As usual, my cerebrations failed to arrive at any meritorious or logical answers so I allowed what I am pleased to call my mind to go back to sleep again, where it would not interfere with my observations of the scenery.

# Of a Day in Summer

Temporary flights of fancy sometimes lead a man to wish he had lived in some other age, when whatever at the moment irks him most had not yet transpired. I so commiserate with myself at times but inevitably wind up overjoyed that I live now when man's knowledge of the universe is so rapidly growing. To participate in and to witness this acquisition of knowledge is such a grand adventure that I can somehow manage to tolerate the ugly aspects of civilization and the reprehensible traits of man so long as I can share the excitement of exploring the heretofore unknown. I suppose, however, my reaction might be the same in any age, long gone, or still to come, since what is old hat now was once new and what is forever yet to come will be entrancingly fresh on arrival. Were it not for the fact that discovery always reveals new goals ahead, fuzzily defined, hazily delineated objectives still to be attained, it would be a discouraging and disheartening event, no matter how momentous at the instant of revelation. Man's chief occupation is the conquest of ignorance, and without the stimulus of this endeavor he would be a sorry creature.

On the outskirts of Cherryfield, several Indians were staggering along under outlandish burdens of trunks, bags, and baskets, looking for a place to live, I guess, while they work on the blueberry barrens.

It was blistering hot now, and I felt listless and uninspired by the time I reached the village. Roger and Don were pouring over a sack of pennies that Don had fetched from the parking meters over at Machias. They showed me one that was a blank planchet, bearing not a trace of the stamping dye. Even this unusual discovery failed to dispel my lethargy—or theirs—for they, too, were feeling the weather.

We gloomily discussed the dearth of salmon in the Pleasant. Roger vowed there was not a fish in the river. Don said there was, because he had heard one splash below the Bridge last evening. Roger said it was a beaver. Don said it wasn't. I said suppose it was a salmon, one fish in twenty-five miles of river didn't offer very bright prospects. So, we relapsed into dismal silence until Roger said that if there were any fish in the river, which there weren't, that the only place they'd be would be above Saco Falls. Don said they couldn't get up 'cause the water was too low and had been for weeks. I said it was too far up there and too hard to get at even if I wanted to go, which I didn't.

So, we looked at each other and out the window at Pineo's truck that was going by, stirring up the dust. Mary —— came down the road with a flock of kids, and I remarked that she looked like an old goose waddling along with her goslings. Don asked Roger which goslings belonged to which gander, and Roger said he didn't know and doubted if Mary did. This was not getting anywhere so I slouched out to the car and slunk in behind the wheel and took off up the river.

A woodchuck dozed at the entrance of his burrow, digesting a bellyful of pre-dawn clover; he was content now to turn the meadow over to the sun-loving bees. The trees drooped in the heat without even a zephyr to fan them.

Somehow or other I arrived at the ridge above Flat Rock and sat there working up enough ambition to amble down the hill to look at the river, and when I did I gulped and looked again and rubbed my eyes and began to shake all over. I counted eight salmon in a thirty-foot stretch of water—every one of them bright

# Of a Day in Summer

and silvery, rolling and rising and swirling around waiting for somebody to drop a fly amongst them.

I jointed up my rod, my hands trembling, and, what with trying to watch the salmon and string the leader through the guides at the same time, I kept missing guides and had to start all over again and again; but finally I made it and managed to get a fly tied on.

I waded in twenty feet below the farthest fish downstream and flipped the dry fly to him, and he smashed into it and tore off upstream. I climbed onto the Flat Rock itself where I could work better; but the fish never stopped going upstream and pretty soon I was tagging along after him, now on the bank, now in the river, back on the bank, and so on. For the first five minutes he did not leap once, but when he did take to the air he was up in it more than he was in the water. I never saw a salmon so air-minded and lost count of his jumps. Every time he did land he went upstream again.

I finally caught up with the salmon just below a spring brooklet that trickles in from the west side. Here, the fish stopped under an overhanging bank and would not budge. I sat down to catch my breath and mop off the sweat. Suddenly the salmon was running again, not fast, just a steady strong run, and came to rest behind a rock at the mouth of the brook where he rolled around in the cold water. Well, the salmon soon took off on a short run and a couple more leaps and then, all at once, gave up, quit altogether and came wallowing over to where I stood in nice clear water.

It was a fine fish, thirty inches long, weighing just ten pounds, and bright as a silver dollar.

I had lunch and took my time about it, watching the smartly tailored waxwings, the skimming barn swallows, and the cottonball clouds. An osprey came hunting along up river and made a successful power dive on a small fish of some kind, ponderously regained altitude, and went flapping off downstream, clutching its prize. I attracted a sizeable school of dace with crumbs of bread; they finally became so stupidly trusting that I caught one in my hand. When released, he dashed off to tell the incredulous others about his marvelous adventure.

# Of a Day in Summer

Some of the underwater stones were studded with globular bryozoan colonies, their transparent jellylike walls painted green with an adhering alga. I watched a damsel fly, *Agrion maculatum*, depositing her eggs on the underside of some pondweed leaves, while the gorgeous male, with brilliant green body and velvety-black wings, fluttered nearby. A big water beetle, probably of the genus *Cybister*, scurried along the bottom between the stems of sagittaria.

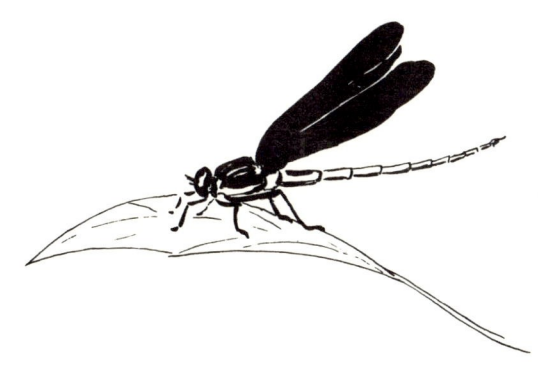

One of the most exciting things about this little planet, this insignificant speck of matter spinning around in its remote corner of the galaxy, is that it is equally mysterious and fascinating whether we view our surroundings through a microscope or a telescope or just peer with unaided vision. I have found it entrancing to examine little patches of the surface of a single cell with an electron microscope, but no more so than I have to survey the surface of the moon with a telescope or to contemplate the wing of a butterfly with my naked eye. There is as much unfathomable mystery in an amoeba as there is in a spiral nebula; a rock is as delightfully inscrutable as Saturn; a snowflake as beautiful as the sea. Everywhere one turns, there are wonderfully intricate patterns of form, balanced and perfect—symphonies of symmetry—coupled exquisitely with incredible functional activities. Everything works. And, when one can no longer look because surfeited with the richness of it all, he can still lose himself in marveling at what is known of its history and development, as revealed by the astronomer, geologist, paleontologist, and anthropologist. All in all, it dwarfs into comical insignificance anything I ever saw in a theater or on a television screen.

The stupendous recent explosion of knowledge about the physical structure of the universe has tended to overshadow the equally great and rapid expansion of knowledge concerning the nature of life, perhaps because of the incredible power within atoms that man has learned to release and the potentialities of which excite, perplex, and frighten him. However, it would be hard to conjure up a more astounding concept than that which has been revealed of the chemical code accounting for the evolution of species and the existence, survival, and reproduction of living forms. No matter how complex the ramifications of the process may appear, the fact remains that the entire stockpile of information that determines the nature of each and every living entity appears to reside in the permutations of only a few variables in the form of those relatively simple molecules, the organic bases, adenosine, cytosine, guanine, and thymine. Upon the linear permutations of these molecules depend the totality of qualities expressed in life and in the specific attributes of the individual. How exquisitely simple and beautifully intricate!

I returned downstream and took the canoe out. Roger has some hives of bees in a clearing near here. I glanced at them as I

drove past and, noticing that one of them was tipped over, went in to investigate, expecting to find bear signs but did not. I guess

# Of a Day in Summer

some pranksters did it. I did observe that there were a lot of dead bees at the entrances of all the hives and decided it was probably due to poisoning from blueberry dust, the chemicals they put on the plants to prevent the blueberry fly from infesting the berries with its maggots.

I dropped in at the Station to tell Roger about the bees. He said bears do not bother the hives until after the wild cherries have gone by. He trapped a bear that was raiding his hives last year; caught it in a big heavy nylon snare but the bear was so strong he tore loose, leaving a deep groove in the side of a tree where the nylon rope gouged into it.

Later, I went with Roger to John ——'s place. Something had dug under the wire fence and killed his chickens and left their corpses scattered around the clearing. John wanted to collect recompense from the State, and Roger, as Selectman, was authorized to attest to the damages. Personally, I suspected John's mongrel as the culprit; he went along with us on the inspection tour, wag-

ging his tail and looking as if he knew what it was all about. I did not say anything because I guess it would be stretching the law a mite to ask the State to cover damages your own dog did, and it was none of my business anyway.

After this matter was taken care of, Roger and I went in to Burnt Mill Rips in his jalopy, which we left in the woods. We came by canoe all the way through to the Village, fishing at likely spots.

We stayed at the Power Line Rips until nearly dark but did not see a fish.

We finally gave up and paddled on downstream through the cool beauty of the night while the whippoorwills called. I arrived at the cottage at eleven, very tired; but any day you catch a salmon is a good day, and this one was good clear through any way you looked at it.

*I was lying on the bank of the river, staring as far out into the cloudless sky as I could. I thought about me and of my fellows on this planet. And then I had a fantasy, or did I doze and dream?*

*From far off in Somewhere, a Being looked down on Earth and scrutinized it, as a microbiologist scanning an agar culture plate bearing colonies of different kinds of bacteria, molds, and fungi. Sweeping over the surface of Earth with the low-power lens of his tele-microscope, he soon remarked the abundance and activity of some strange little organisms running around on their hind legs. He was impressed with their rapid increase and their flourishing colonies, and he smiled and switched over to his high-power lens and focused it upon one of these colonies, in order to study it in greater detail, and he was enraptured with what he saw.*

*He was astonished at the furious energy and ceaseless enterprise of these creatures as they darted in and out of their honeycombs, floated about on little chips in the liquid parts of the medium, whizzed through the air above in winged machines, and rolled along over the dry areas in streaming lines of still other machines, born on spinning discs. He marveled at the ingenuity, the cleverness, of these organisms. He saw them cluster into groups and then disperse, only to cluster again. He looked in awe at all of the beautiful things and harkened to the lovely sounds they created; and he noted that they worshipped, cared for their sick and injured, and tended their young. They were compassionate loving things, filled with sympathy and lofty ideals, and he smiled and said, "How wonderful! How incredibly wonderful! What wonderful little organisms these are!"* And he went on looking.

He saw that they squabbled at times and even became quite violent in their quarrels, that they fought furious battles with other colonies. Here were some of them making a great to-do about what color they were. "How amusing," he said. "Aren't they the strange little things!" But then he became entranced again with their other occupations. "Why, look there! The little rascals are actually throwing pieces of their culture medium right out into Space, even so far as to hit that Star that incubates them! Fantastic! My, what ingenuity they have! But they're *increasing so fast. Their colonies are expanding at such a rate that they're crowding all the other kinds of organisms off the plate. If they keep on at such a pace, they'll soon run out of nutrient medium, as well as have no room to move about. I wonder what will happen to them?"*

*And then an expression of confusion, of utter bafflement swept over his face. Then a look of horror. He suddenly realized that the* bulk of the little creatures' energy and resources were being directed to the building of terrible engines of destruction—solely, exquisitely, conscientiously designed for the specific purpose of annihilating themselves! *His face clouded with anger and disgust, and he shuddered. "This is unbelievable! The gruesome beasts! I will reach down with my spatula and scrape off each and every one of their ghastly colonies before they destroy not only themselves but all else on the culture plate as well."*

*And then he shook his head and smiled again. "Ah no," he said. "This is ridiculous, preposterous! What a fool I am! No living thing could possibly work to such a stupid grisly purpose, least of all this* extraordinarily intelligent *organism. No, I have made a silly mistake, of course. To think I might have destroyed them! No, I'll let them be. They deserve more study. Surely, though, astounding things are soon going to take place down there. I'll return to them later and see what happens."* He shook his head. *"It just could not be,"* he said, and turned his tele-microscope away to observe other culture plates elsewhere in the Universe.

*I was lying on the bank of the river, looking far out into the sky, and now a great billowing cloud rose up from behind the trees, and in the distance I heard the rumbling of thunder.*

*Or* was it thunder?

11

## To the Source of the Pleasant

I did not arrive at the Village until early afternoon, having stopped off at the Narraguagus to cast over a blissfully indifferent salmon basking in the Cable Pool. While driving on eastward, it occurred to me, as it had intermittently in the past, that although I had dawdled away a half-dozen summers on the Pleasant I had never seen its source, a lake of the same name tucked far back in the spruce-clad hills.

Except for its extreme upper part, I was now well acquainted with the stream's entire course to the sea. The upper reaches had fascinated me as far as I had probed them, because the country grew considerably wilder as it became more difficult of access. My farthest ramblings upstream had been in the canoe, paddling the long, twisting deadwater stretches through dense forest and past boggy intervales with quiet logans here and there and an abundance of botanical delights. In such a place, I had come upon a cow moose accompanied by her two-year-old bull calf the summer before. These journeys had carried me well above the entrance of Heath Brook, to the foot of a piece of quick water. Beyond this, I had not as yet ventured.

I consulted Roger, knowing that I would need his help in finding my way. It required little persuasion to enlist his participation in the venture since he, too, was attracted by the untrammeled nature of this section of the country. We pored over some

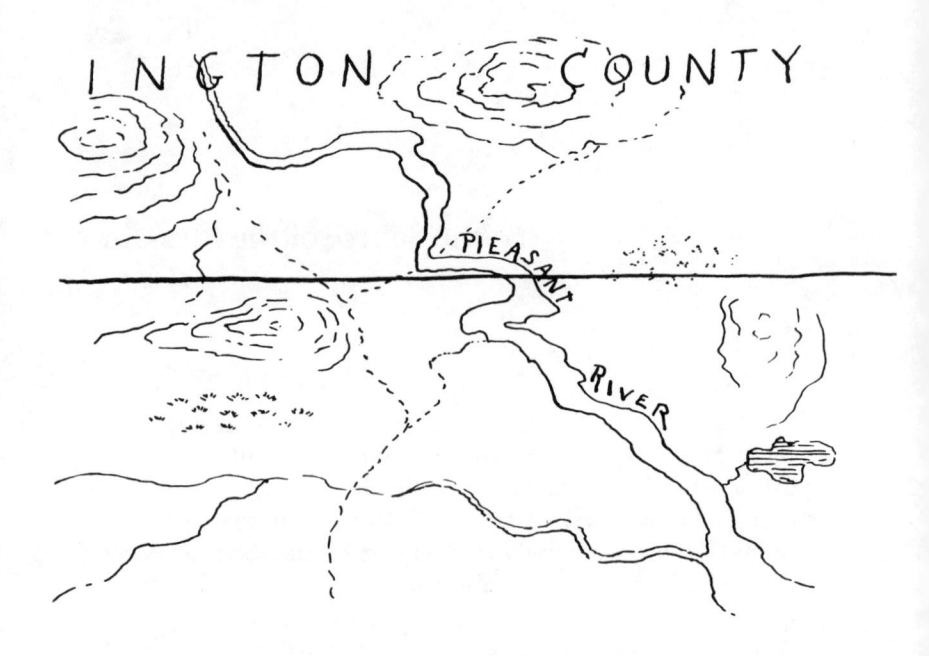

maps and decided to try to reach the lake by going up the west side of the valley, keeping as close to the river as possible. We judged it to be twenty miles or so in a straight line. The usual way to go to the lake would be to return to Cherryfield and take a road that intersects the "air-line" route between Bangor and Calais. A good dirt road then leads more or less directly to the lake that lies only a short distance south.

However, we wanted to stay as near to the river as possible all the way up. Roger said that when he was a boy his father had taken him on trips up the west side, but they had never gone all

## To the Source of the Pleasant

the way to the lake. The maps indicated the existence of two possible trails to our destination, though whether either would prove passable there was no way of knowing until we tried.

We had no time to lose; so we picked up some sandwiches and were soon jouncing along over the winding sandy roads across the vast blueberry barrens, stirring up huge clouds of dust behind us.

The barrens here have a few trees, isolated tall red pines that tower over the rolling plains looking strangely grotesque and other-worldly, reminiscent in some way of the Joshua trees of the south-western deserts or like scattered palms on broad savannahs.

The ground is covered with a dense growth of low-bush blueberries, sweet fern, and sheep laurel, or lambkill. Roger says the barrens have always been this way, though they have been extended in some areas by lumbering and burning to encourage the growth of blueberries. Evidently, the soil is not suitable to support a forest.

As we reached the crest of the plateaulike hills, we could see Mount Cadillac's familiar form poking up from the southern horizon, looking much closer than the thirty miles distant we knew it to be. For mile upon mile, the barrens rolled away in all directions, ending only in the blue distance where a narrow dark rim of forest touched the sky.

At intervals, several miles apart, we drove through clusters of tar-paper shacks, provided as shelter for the Indians while employed as berrypickers. These crude dwellings were occupied now by Micmacs from Big Cove, Nova Scotia, the harvest being in full swing. The physical characteristics of these people were strikingly attractive, the men tall and lithe with handsome features, the young women with well-formed bodies and pretty faces. Their skin was smooth, reddish brown and the hair quite black and straight. But I was saddened by the poverty apparent in their torn shabby clothes and tattered shoes. Also, their countenances were sullen, and their eyes seemed to express scorn and distrust as I looked into their faces. They did not return my smiles or greetings. It rankled me to see these original occupants of the land forced, by the imposition of our economic system, to pick the white man's berries for him at so much a bushel—men, women, and children—berries to which, it seemed to me, the Indians had a more just and ancient claim than that testified to by scraps of paper in the Town Clerk's office.

I was angered at the huts they were housed in, mean structures devoid of mosquito netting or screens and rudely equipped with cheap, broken chairs and cots. There was, of course, no running water, plumbing, or electricity. I have seen hogs in better circumstances and was torn between deep despair and fuming fury. For once I felt justified in giving free vent to both loathing and shame for my greedy mercenary brethren of the pallid skin. My heart ached for the children especially, and I longed for some great revelation that would point the way to a happier future for them, but no satisfactory solution was forthcoming. I was glad when we had passed through the last of these abject communities and were required to concentrate on the problem of finding our way across the wilder barrens we were now entering, but I think I shall not live so long as to forget these Indian people.

One of our possible courses was a dimly defined trail crossing a tributary of the Pleasant designated as Bog Stream, so we searched for its valley. We came out upon a higher knoll than the other nearby ones and from this vantage point could look down on the Pleasant flowing slowly through a stand of alders and aspens and retarded by several beaver dams. Roger decided to hike down to the river, a quarter mile off, and make a few casts for trout or salmon. I chose to stay behind not having been able to fully shake off the depression evoked by the Indians and wanting to set my mind at peace alone.

I sought an outcropping of rock for a seat and swept the miles of landscape with field glasses hoping to discover a bear or moose but had to settle for two deer a mile or more away, their summer-red coats standing out against the dull greenish-gray background. Two ravens wheeled high over the barrens and, to more keenly savor the wonder of their flight, I lay on my back, restricting the encompass of my view to only the sky and the birds. Thus observed, it seemed as though the ravens soared through an illuminated bottomless sea, their gliding black forms etched against the deep blue of the awesome depths. The loneliness of the birds in this endless abyss was appealing. I followed them until lost in the distance and then roused myself to gather blueberries from the heavily burdened bushes about me.

While picking berries, I fell to wondering, as often, as to how I should like most to spend my life—or what is left of it. Its brevity stands in saddening conflict with the countless delightful possibilities. One starts eliminating, but it is depressing to consciously eliminate a single aliquot from all conceivable adventures in living. As daily fare, it is better to enjoy each morsel as one comes to it than to dwell upon what banquets or feasts may lie ahead. The occasional moments of reflection and the taking stock of past and probable future events are inescapable, but fruitless.

By the time Roger returned, I had filled my battered felt hat nearly to the brim with berries. We set them between us on the seat of the car and ate them by handfuls as we pushed on to the north.

We found the semblance of a trail bearing to the right and, deciding to follow it, soon found ourselves descending a steep and badly eroded hillside filled with gullies that required the four-wheel-drive mechanism of the Jeep to negotiate. This proved to be the valley of Bog Stream, but, when we reached its bottom, we found the old plank bridge caved in and unpassable while a beaver dam below elevated the water level so that we could not ford the stream; a beaver swimming across it was placidly unperturbed by our predicament.

We finally managed to turn around and clawed and scrambled back up the hillside where we took the other trail that stayed with the high ground. From here, we could look out over the valley of the Pleasant to the barrens beyond, familiar to us as those that rolled on eastward to the Machias River. It was as though we had a huge topographic map laid out before us.

Having made this survey, we pressed on north and west, aided by the compass on the dash as the sky had now clouded over. The land became more wild in appearance. The declivities were sharper with rugged outcroppings of gray rock forming ledges and jagged peaks jutting above the undergrowth. Gradually the trees became more numerous and taller and before long we were following an almost obliterated path through heavy forest.

We penetrated a swamp where some of the cedars had boles two feet in diameter. I noticed some fine big balsam firs. The trunks of both yellow and white birches glistened wanly in the gloomy light. Long festoons of Usnea hung from the twigs and branches of spruces, affording countless possible homes for parula warblers in their nesting season. An occasional circular moss-covered mass indicated where once a giant white pine had been felled so that we were not surprised to come upon the decaying remains of a long-abandoned lumber camp, its doorless and unglazed openings staring with vacant eyes at our intrusion into this years-silent realm. Man's furious labor and enterprise, I thought, rotting into oblivion behind him. The noble pines decimated, man departed, jingling some coins in his pocket and leaving his hovels and scars behind. I was glad to see the forest reclaiming its own.

The faint trail led on and on. It began to rain. We had about reached the grim conclusion that our venture was a failure and were debating what to do. If we turned around, could we retrace our path in the darkness that would soon fall? If not, what were our prospects on further progress northward? Would the trail continue to be passable? It was difficult to follow now and seemed to be getting more densely overgrown with each hundred yards of travel. And then, we bounced out of a thicket onto a dirt road, a well-traveled one.

This time we chose to turn left and abruptly arrived at the

Fish Hatchery!—usually reached by coming in from Deblois. We stopped at the hatchery and watched some captive Atlantic salmon that were being held in a constructed pool until their eggs were mature for stripping, fertilization, and artificial rearing. They were pitiful to see—dark in color and with ugly patches of fungus growing on their backs and sides—a deplorable contrast with the silvery-blue fish in the rivers.

The attendant came out of his cottage to chat, an opportunity evidently not often available to him, and he obviously relished it and made the most of it, since it was difficult to stem his flow. We asked if we could reach Pleasant River Lake by going on up the valley. He said it might be possible in the Jeep, but we would surely have trouble finding our way and night would almost certainly overtake us before we got through—if we could get through. He was much surprised to learn that we had been able to traverse the country we had, and this seemed to give him some confidence we could make it the rest of the way if we did not become lost. He gave us some vague directions to start on and we left.

It was rough going. There were many sharp hills to climb and descend, and the trail consisted only of a pair of ill-defined ruts hidden by undergrowth and branches. Saplings grew in the mid-

# To the Source of the Pleasant

dle here and there but none so large we could not bend them down and pass over. We twisted and turned, jounced and joggled along, seldom able to see more than a few feet beyond the hood of the car. This continued for mile after slow mile. Now and again the path would branch, and we could only hope we chose correctly.

In the low, damp places, cinnamon fern grew in heavy ranks, taller and more luxuriant than usual. I was surprised to see several rose pogonias still in bloom at so late a date. They looked wistful, maybe for lack of appreciation in such a remote place. There were many thick carpets of lycopodium, or club moss. Birds were few, the whitethroat, of course, and chickadees. From a dead tree in a small clearing, an olive-sided flycatcher drunkenly called for

"Hic - three beers!" Red squirrels chattered at us as we progressed from the bounds of one's territory into the next. These were the only mammals we saw.

We came out on a road again—a dirt road, but fairly well worn. After studying the lay of the land, we concluded that by following the road westward we should come to the lake whereas the other way we should probably cross the Pleasant River a short distance below its source. Gambling on this decision, we turned left and within a mile, sure enough, came out on the shore of Pleasant River Lake. We had made it. A big porcupine came shambling down the trail to greet us but would not tarry to have me take his picture. He rustled off into the dripping brush through which

I had no inclination to follow. The rain had become a steady downfall now.

Where we touched the lake shore, a broad sandy beach shelved off gradually into a shallow bay where yellow pond lilies grew in some profusion. There were a few hunting camps discernible on the shores, but the only current resident of the area was a loon that acknowledged our arrival with his wavering cry. The lake appeared to be about two and a half miles long and half or three-quarters of a mile wide, surrounded by spruce forest. Roger said it was stocked with land-locked salmon.

We strolled along the sandy beach, noting numerous deer tracks as well as the handlike patterns of a raccoon's footprints. On a smooth stone, there were some muskrat droppings. We studied the shore line carefully and finally descried the dam over which the lake spills its water to produce the Pleasant River. Except for the loon's periodic tremulous call, it was quiet, and the lovely desolation of the place was augmented by the monotonous rain and the rapidly failing light. I was reluctant to leave.

We retraced our path and then took the road eastward, finding that it soon swung in a more northerly direction. We had gone only a short way when we came upon a wooden bridge spanning a stream of some eight or ten feet in width. We got out to inspect it and suddenly realized that it was the Pleasant River, though Pleasant Brook would seem a more appropriate appellation at this youthful stage of its existence. From this point, it could only be a quarter mile or less upstream to the dam and, as we traveled on, the road that must lead to it branched off to the left. However, much as we both were eager to see the dam at close hand, night was now upon us so we postponed the visit for another day's adventure.

The road became smooth and easy now, passing through spruce woods and open clearings. Several deer revealed themselves by the shine of their eyes in our headlights, and one fine buck dashed across the road just ahead of us.

We knew that this road must bring us out onto the "air-line" highway, and when it did Roger was able to pinpoint our location. The Machias River passes under the highway a hundred yards to

# To the Source of the Pleasant

the east while the bridge over the Narraguagus River lies only a few miles west. Thus all three rivers here come within a relatively short distance from each other, though each runs in its own valley.

We drove down to Cherryfield and then back eastward to the Village where we parted, both of us regretting that our explorations had come to an end.

I was tired but still had an hour's drive to the cottage. I felt a great contentment that I had now traced the Pleasant to its source. I decided that though I held its entire length in deep affection my special fancy was for these untamed parts that I had just visited. I conjured up fantasies of building there a log cabin wherein to live a hermit's life in my declining years, while drawing together a complete journal of my inconsequential, but thoroughly relished, sojourn on the planet.

*Got a extry brown hackle fly, Jim?*
*Sure, Sim, here's some. Help yourself.*
*Huh. Ain't none of 'em worth a damn. Hooks is too small fer the length o' hackle. Tails had oughta be red. And longer. Heads too big, too. You'd oughta wound in more hackle, Jim; too light ta float good. I'll take this one, but it ain't much of a fly. Pretty poor, take it all an' all. I wouldn't gen'rally use such a fly myself.*
*Well, here. Give it back then, Sim. I ain't tryin' ta force it on ya.*
*Oh, it's okay. It'll hafta do. I'll make out with it somehow ruther.*
*Then what ya runnin' it down so fer, Sim?*
*Well, it's like this, Jim. If I should lose this here fly in the alders now, ya can't say as how ya lost much. If I don't take a salmon on it, it certainly ain't my fault—it's yourn—and if I* do *take a salmon on it, it jest goes to show how good a fisherman I am. Wanted to set the picture straight, that's all, so there wouldn't be no argyin' 'bout it later on. Thanks fer the louzy fly, Jim. See ya later.*

# 12

## Of Toads and Truants, Sinners and Savants

I sat on a grassy hilltop this afternoon, just at the edge of the Village whose white spire poked above the cluster of rooftops showing through the trees. The Pleasant River wound sleepily below, bordered by a few shabby shacks where the smelt nets are stored and by a piece of marsh spread out like a carpet between the stream and the spruce-covered hills that enclose the valley.

Since early dawn, I had been casting flies for salmon. Now, in the warm sunlight of a lazy summer day, I looked below and thought about contentedly inconsequential matters. After a while however, I became aware of a strange sadness. I felt a longing for something forever lost, my boyhood, of course, but more than that, its most appealing element—the provincial.

If provincialism is actually a vice, I thought, it is one that has the allure of easy acquisition, like most vices, and a man of weak character might be excused for harboring a desire to desist from his tense efforts to attain supposedly loftier standards and a broader outlook and to wallow in the delights of sinning a little; but, if provincialism is conducive to true peace, it deserves scrutiny and consideration, for the loss of peace is a high price to pay for the attainment of any other objectives.

I pictured the inhabitants of the village—Roger Wakefield, with telegraph and bills of lading in his office on the Maine Central; Sim, Lloyd and Ken Driscoll, at the Town Market; Pat Oliver and his pulpwood operations; Roger Fickett, in his garage; Don Higgins, pondering upon the outlaws; the outlaws scheming to set a net tonight; the postmaster; boys on bikes; teenagers courting. This is provincial, all right; and, in all my comings and goings in the valley, I recall little being said about Communism, race relations, atomic energy, or space explorations.

It was in such surroundings that I grew up. Here on the hilltop, it came flooding back for a few nostalgic moments. Forty-five years ago, I might well have skipped school this afternoon and rested here, contemplating the drowsy hamlet below, while preparing my feeble defenses for having played hooky. I saw myself, on foot or bike, going from home to the Schoolhouse, or to the Store, or Post office, or cutting school to go a-fishing, or just to loaf away a pretty afternoon on a hilltop blessed with clover and daisies, lulled by the hum of honeybees.

I was mildly shocked to suddenly realize that I had a kinship

# Of Toads and Truants, Sinners and Savants

even with the outlaws, for I, too, had shot deer out of season and had jigged a pickerel or two in my time, had roamed the woods, swamps, and marshes, usually toting a gun, and was not averse to killing for the sake of killing, and once, when in need of a chicken while camping, had raided a farmer's coop for one, wrung its neck, and thoroughly relished the excitement of my outlawry. I had poached on private streams, had hunted on posted property, and the exhilarating awareness of my guilt had enhanced my sport considerably.

I realized that part of my wistfulness this afternoon was attributable to the fact that I could no longer sin in such a delectable fashion. At some stage during the years, I had, all unwittingly, passed over to the other side. I had accepted the stern dictates of lawfulness and compassion, was now used to them, proclaimed them, and was so biased and bigoted as to denounce all others who did not do likewise. I had undergone a complete about face in my prejudices and had almost forgotten my previous sins only to discover myself sinning in the opposite direction. It was evident that my sympathy and understanding must do some more growing up.

In those earlier days, the world consisted essentially of the village and its surrounding forests, swamps, marshes, brooks, bays, and the adjacent seacoast. The great men in my life were the School Superintendent, the Doctor, the Storekeeper, the Truant Officer, the Dog Catcher, and my Father, none of whose stations in life I aspired to assume. My heroes were a lobsterman, a local expert on trout fishing, a trapper with genuine Indian blood, and a tousle-headed entrancingly disreputable renegade who lived as a hermit back in the hills with a rifle and a pack of hound-dogs. The momentous yearly events were the closing of school in spring, the Decoration Day parade, the Fourth of July, Christmas, and the opening of fishing and hunting seasons. The great tragedies were the taking up of school in the fall, the night Mrs. Brown committed suicide, the day John Gould's house and barn burned down, when one of my dogs was run over, the spring afternoon a chum was drowned; but even these direful events did not bog down my ebullient spirits for long.

My life was one of toads and turtles, deer and ducks, trout and bass, skipping school, camping out, wet feet, dogs, green ap-

ples—and fantasies. I knew vaguely that the land stretched on and on, as did the sea, and that there were big cities and foreign countries; but all of these were more like fairy tales and the illustrations in picture books than actualities and were of no real significance because so remote.

There were chores—slopping the hogs, feeding the chickens, gathering eggs, cleaning the barn, lugging scuttles of coal for the kitchen stove, stoking the furnace, taking out the ashes, shoveling snow—nuisances, irksome but tolerable. School was an annoyance,

## Of Toads and Truants, Sinners and Savants

a compulsory inconvenience, but not of enough moment to interfere seriously with sailing, hay rides, and mumblety-peg.

Nor did the adults around me seem much concerned with the outside world; their interests, as mine, were local, provincial. The weather, crops, churches, schools, and the fortunes and misfortunes, births, illnesses, and deaths of fellow townsmen—these were the burden of thought and conversation. The "government", state or federal, was way off somewhere and mostly, I gathered, did everything wrong and cost too much. Town Meeting was more immediate and pertinent to our affairs.

This was provincialism all right. I had forgotten how delightful it was until this afternoon when I sat on the crest of the hill and looked down into the valley of the Pleasant.

This, then, was why I sensed beneath the appealing calm a longing and a sadness. My provincialism and youth were victims of the passing years and exposure to the atmospheres of other regions. Had I stayed in the village, I might have retained my provincialism if not my youth. Having lost provincialism, I have substituted for the complacent bliss of my boyhood the disquieting knowledge that has come through years of exposure to prickling contacts with scholars in all fields. The savants completely wrecked my happily carefree little world. For my boyhood friends, I substituted those probing minds in the forefront of man's conquest over his primitive origins and over the universe he inhabits, though I find myself somewhat discomfited amid such erudite company.

Perhaps all fly-fishermen are merely striving to regain their boyhood. Maybe we are not in quest of trout and salmon so much as we are seeking an unruffled, bucolic way of life, having grown weary with the harassments, the frictions, the frustrations that confront and surround us in our other lives. Maybe this is true of at least some of us who have never quite grown up after all and were not truly of the sort to have gone abroad to face the world and to take it in stride but, having inadvertently done so, must return for solace and healing to the cool springs from which we sipped as youngsters and to bathe again in the refreshing pool of simplicity, peace—and provincialism.

Which man am I really? Both, I suppose, and perhaps one

neither more nor less than the other. I feel happily at home here in the valley of the Pleasant. Its people are my people, and I can comfortably join and mingle with them, understand and be understood by them. I get along with them and they with me, easily, without effort. We speak a common language and, while I am here, share common viewpoints, motivations, and interests. Here, I am the original native me and, when I depart to enter the other world that I inhabit, I am the fabricated, molded, acquired me and have now worn my new clothes long enough that I am not too painfully chafed by them, however much I rebelled during the long process of trying them on.

This afternoon I wished with all my heart that I could return to this kind of environment from which I took origin and slip into some available niche where I might contentedly bask once again in an out-of-the-way puddle of rusticity and serenity—that serenity I saw and felt as I looked down into the valley of the Pleasant, thinking of a boy that used to be, quite a long time ago. I am not sure that I do not still so wish but, when I picture myself doing it, I feel a strange rankling within, a vague sense of fear suggests that I might thereafter forever be chastising myself for having skipped the school of world affairs and for having adopted perpetual truancy as a way of life—or do I flatter myself on the depth of my veneer of sophistication?

I am about resigned that I must settle for the nostalgic pleasures of such reveries as I have permitted myself this afternoon and accept the compromise of only vacationing in peace and provincialism. This much, thankfully, my conscience will accept without quaking, and I can also allow myself to reflect now and then upon what might have been. I cannot shake off, however, the disturbing thought that the price paid, in terms of composure and tranquillity, has been so high as to make my meager achievements and contributions appear as trifling recompense. I wish—I am not quite sure what I wish.

*Any fish in, Joe?*
*Dunno.*
*Well, haven't you seen any?*
*No. I ain't seen none.*
*Has anybody else seen any?*
*Ain't only asked them as I've run inta. They ain't.*
*Then what are you fishing for?*
*Cuz I ain't swum the hull river* lookin', *and I ain't asked* ever'body.

# 13

## One of Those Days

The coffee boiled over and cascaded onto the stove and floor. I forgot to take the cup that screws onto the top of the thermos; the cork leaked and the sandwich eagerly absorbed the coffee; a promising start. It looked like one of those days, and I debated whether to carry through with it or go back to bed, with the inevitable result.

Black ducks were dabbling on the clam flats near the Twinnies and off Thomas Island. Scattered yellowlegs and black-bellied plovers were wading in the shallows, and here and there a great blue heron stood statuesquely still. Ken Johnson chugged up the bay in his lobster boat, towing a flock of milling gulls. The old white horse, on the back-road shortcut, gazed solemnly at the dawn from the barn window. Tom Clarke's Guernseys, all pointing in the same direction, grazed in the meadow. A flock of green-winged teal were tippling at Mud Run. Two ravens flew from the road near Route 1.

A farmer was dragging a plow behind his tractor, preparing the soil for next year's planting and seeming to entertain no doubt as to what he was about. I have never been certain as to what I wanted to grow in my own garden. I have hoed a lot of rows. The crops produced have been neither excellent nor inferior. I am running short on seeds and seasons now and might become frenetic about the prospects if I paused to dwell upon it; that is, if I ever stopped looking and dreaming and started thinking.

Cherryfield was just waking up; Colby unlocking his gasoline pumps; Ken Oakes setting out on his mail route; Harry Smith going to, or coming from, some place in his Jeep truck. It started me thinking about Norm Morse—they found him dead in the snow in March, rifle in his hands, snowshoes on, back at his camp where he was hunting wildcats with his two hounds. The young dog came out after a few days, but the old one stayed with Norm's body for the ten days before it was found. I miss Norm; I am sure everybody does, but especially Leola, of course.

Arriving at the Pleasant, I drove up to Saco Falls and tramped in to some pools I know about and, though I have not taken a salmon from them yet, would rather not say just where they are. There was a salmon in the first pool, a really big one, and I worked hard for two hours with dry flies without results, and then the fish swirled around and bolted upstream, all for no apparent reason. I am hesitant to say just how big this fish was but would be surprised if it would go less than thirty pounds, not that most people would believe me, and maybe that is just as well. Roger says never hesitate to tell the truth about fishing on the Pleasant because nobody will believe you anyhow and that way you can stay honest and still not reveal any secrets.

Authors of fishing books and articles, when considering a fish that is difficult to catch, endow the prey with that quality man recognizes as his own highest attainment—superior intelligence. I find it difficult—and humiliating—to bestow upon a trout or salmon, with its pea-sized brain, an intelligence beyond my own. I prefer to believe that if the fish had the capacity to think and act in any way comparable to me, I would have little trouble outwitting it. It succeeds in eluding me, a man, only because of its very lack of intelligence and its dependence upon piscine reflexes to stimuli that bestir it to react in the only way that so stupid a thing as a fish can react. Adoption of this viewpoint lends a certain comforting satisfaction to being unable to catch a fish.

I never cease to marvel at the Atlantic salmon. This fish begins life as an egg deposited in one of several depressions excavated by the female in the gravelly riverbed. The egg is fertilized by the attending male. About seven hundred eggs are shed for each pound the female weighs and the eggs are covered by coarse gravel to which they adhere. Spawning usually takes place in October and November, and the eggs hatch to produce alevins within ninety to one hundred and twenty days, depending upon the water temperature. The baby salmon usually spends two years as a parr in the river, though this varies with individuals from one to several years. The parr feed voraciously on insects and other aquatic life. During this period, the young fish are colored like trout, brownish-green backs and with bright red spots on their sides. Before running to sea, as smolts, the trout colors are replaced by the silvery sides, blue back, black spots, and white bellies of the adult salmon, the camouflage colors of marine fishes. The silvery color is due to guanine.

It is not known just where salmon congregate in the sea, though it is presumably in the North Atlantic, perhaps under the ice cap. Fish tagged in the Narraguagus River have been recovered off the coast of Greenland. In the marine environment, the salmon grow rapidly on a diet of prawns and capelins and other fish and crustaceans. After one, two, or several years in the ocean, the adult fish return, almost invariably to the river of origin, in order to repeat the cycle. A fish that spends no more than thirteen months in the salt water is called a *grilse*. As soon as the salmon enter the fresh water, they cease feeding altogether, even though their fast may be of many months' duration. They lose weight, turn gradually darker in color, and are nearly exhausted by the time spawning is completed. Many of these kelts, or "black salmon," die or fall easy prey to eels, otters, and other enemies. Those that manage to survive return to the healing waters of the sea, where they grow even larger. Such fish will return again to spawn. Five spawning runs have been recorded for an individual, though this is most unusual.

Most of the fish caught in the rivers of Maine are "two-two" fish, meaning that they have spent two years in the river as parr and two years at sea and are making their first spawning run when taken. Their average weight is then in the neighborhood of ten pounds with considerable individual variation. The life history of the fish is written upon its scales, much like the growth rings of trees, and it is not difficult to learn to "read" the scales. I find it an interesting wintertime occupation to decipher the life histories of the fish I have caught the past summer.

The salmon fisherman is thus confronted with an unusual problem for anglers. He fishes for a fish that is not feeding. It is not known for certain why the salmon will occasionally take an artificial fly; the most acceptable theory is that the fly awakens a dormant reflex that once gave the parr sustenance when in the same environment. Salmon can be seen to take natural insects from the surface at times but evidently they then spit them out

## One of Those Days

because their stomachs are invariably empty and shrunken when examined.

It is a fortunate provision that salmon do not feed when in the rivers since the hordes of incoming fish would soon exhaust the supply of edible material in the river, including parr.

The alewives, smelt, and lampreys are also anadromous fish, spawning in the fresh water and sojourning the rest of the time in salt water, whereas the common eel is catadromous, living in fresh water and going to sea to spawn. How did such strange cycles become established?

Knowledge about something brings a sense of gratification and the satiation of a thirsting curiosity; it also prepares the mind for the acquisition of more knowledge, leading to greater understanding. But, knowledge also begets complacency, even boredom, whereas mystery, the unsolved, whets excitement and wonderment. Knowledge may at times close the doors that mystery holds ajar. Fortunately, however, facts are but *temporary* truths; and doors, once confidently shut, spring wide again in the future, when some restless curiosity has chosen to probe further and to question what was supposedly fully known and comfortably closeted.

I returned to the car and drove up the east side to a clearing where I parked and then slipped and skidded down the steep bank to the river. There was a salmon in a slick between two rocks. The first drift of a dingy gray-brown dry fly bestirred the salmon, and I thought I had fastened when all went loose. Upon examin-

ing the hook, I found that the point was broken off, and then I remembered the coffee boiling over, the forgotten cup, and the soggy sandwich and was not surprised. It *was* that kind of a day, and there was not a thing to do about it now but see it through somehow and hope I did not break my rod or a leg before it ended.

I struggled back up the bank. There is something honest and dependable about a big oak tree. I have noticed the same thing about a coil of good rope, too.

I did not flicker an eyelash at the flat tire on the right rear; just pulled out the jack and, very, very carefully, raised the wheel and put on the spare and was consternated to find that it had air in it. I ate the soggy sandwich and drank the coffee straight from the bottle; then had a smoke on my pipe and set off, sort of resigned and philosophical, meek and cautious—but realistic enough to be expectant.

The whine of a chain saw always depresses my spirits—fills me with gloom. It takes so long to make a tree. It does not take long, however, to convert one into a paper bag, the want-ad section of the Bangor Daily News, or a roll of toilet tissue—to throw into the incinerator or flush down the drain. I have a strong aversion to chain saws and bulldozers and look upon them as evil weapons of destruction, hideously ugly in themselves, cunningly designed for the ruthless annihilation of beautiful things. To some people, they may mean a living, but I am entitled to my opinion. Unreasonable and reactionary though it may be, I still prefer even a very small sapling to a box of Kleenex.

Sometimes as I stand at the edge of a forest, I am overwhelmed with depression. It seems that from everywhere before me comes the snarl of chain saws, crashing of trees, and the coughing of bulldozers gouging gaping furrows through the mantle of living things, while from close behind I hear the roar and rumble of stone, concrete, asphalt, and steel, sweeping over the land as a monstrous tidal wave that no barriers can withstand. I stand there trembling with no place left to go, no silent sylvan sanctuary of light and shadow, no sun-flooded clearing with birds and blossoms, no clean cool waters gliding between grassy banks. How few there are who stand there with me and how futile the wish to block the avalanche—burgeoning masses, lust and greed, utter indifference.

At the Alders, above Arty's Bridge, two salmon were lying

## One of Those Days

side by side in the quick water. One of them splashed at a Mackintosh and then sought the deep water. I may have pricked him. The other salmon would rise when my fly was in the air on the back cast and sink when it drifted over the fish, no matter how I timed it. Then I flubbed a cast that landed three feet to the right, and the salmon dashed over and grabbed it as though he had been waiting for it for months.

As soon as I set the hook, the salmon shot into the air, turned end over end and landed on its side with a huge splash, leaped again, falling on its back, and then up again in a long slanting sidewise jump, skidding into the water and tearing off downstream. In spite of all this grand commotion, I remained remarkably calm and unmoved because, in view of the fact that it *was* that kind of day, I took it for granted the episode would eventually end dismally. It was just a matter of waiting until it was time to reel in, stare glumly at the busted leader, and depart. As a matter of fact, I became irritated when the fish stayed on and kept peeling off line because it only meant that much more to reel in when the break came and delayed the agonizing climax that I was anxious to put behind me.

But, the minutes went by and the fish kept running, leaping, sulking, and doing all the things a salmon should do to get loose and yet I remained fast. I finally worked the fish into the quiet water and brought it into gaffing range. Still, I thought it futile to slip the leather guard off the gaff, knowing full well it was tempting the Furies beyond reason and hating to let them think they were deluding me into any hopeful expectations.

However, when the salmon seemed utterly exhausted and lolling quietly on its side three feet in front of me, I could resist no longer and pulled off the guard, grabbed the handle, placed the big hook carefully just beyond the fish and drew it toward me

with a sudden surge of confidence. The salmon turned, ever so little but just enough that the gaff slipped by, picked up the leader, and neatly plucked out the fly. I could hear the Furies shrieking in gales of crazy laughter as the salmon swam slowly into the slick and disappeared; but, after the first shuddering quake, I assumed a nonchalant air and gathered in my tackle, though I guess my fingers were still trembling, and I was all limp inside, but hoped the Furies would not notice it and would be disappointed that they had not disturbed me.

I threaded my way through the alders and came to the little rivulet that has cut itself a deep channel through the clay bank. I carefully poked my rod through a gap in the alders and then cautiously stepped across, but my foot slipped and I slumped into the rivulet, all in a heap. It happened so suddenly I had no time to throw the rod free and I heard that sickening, crackling sound of splintering Tonkin cane. The fractured tip dangled dismally before my eyes. I did not even have the spirit to fill the air with curses and lamentations, just slowly climbed out of the slippery, gooey mixture of clay and water and trudged resignedly to the car. I glanced furtively at the spare tire. It was still inflated so I climbed in and drove slowly and carefully down to the Station to see Roger. I had had enough fishing and decided it would be wiser to place myself in someone else's hands before I broke my neck.

**One of Those Days** 157

Later, I went with Roger down to the mouth of the river in his jalopy to pick up some hives he had rented out for pollinating blueberries. The farms looked even poorer in this lower part of the valley and many of them were deserted.

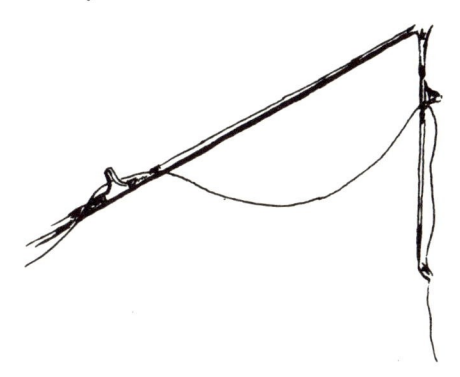

The hives were located on a hillside from which the village of South Addison was visible, as well as the slowly flowing tidal part of the Pleasant. The country rolled gently seaward, and her-

ring gulls wheeled overhead, screaming that the coast was close by. The trees tossed their heads saucily in a fresh breeze. While

Roger lugged the hives, now heavy with honey, and loaded them into his jalopy, I gorged myself with blueberries and scenery. I explored the fields for botanical discoveries but came upon nothing remarkable.

What a preposterous statement! As though a blade of grass, a wisp of chickweed, or a toadstool were not a sheer miracle! Common they may be so far as their numbers go, but man is common too, and I have no doubt he would heartily resent my stating that I had found him but passed him by as nothing remarkable. The lowly chickweed has no doubt dwelt upon this planet for longer than has my kind, watched the earth change with the centuries and changed with it as necessary for survival. What more, *basically*, has man done?

Oh, to know the world as all other living things know it! I am restricted to so narrow a view. I watch a chickadee. I see it feed its young, seek shelter from a storm, preen its feathers in the sun. I see it look at me. But I know nothing whatever of a chickadee's world from a chickadee's viewpoint, the only meaningful viewpoint. Here I wander, noting this and that, missing most, passing opinions, drawing conclusions, and priding myself upon my knowledge of the world in which I live; I, who can see with only a hazy and bewildered vision, and mine only. A snail does as much but keeps his counsel.

I drove home at dark, thinking back over the day; and it was only when I was sitting in the tub, with my pipe and a glass of brandy, that I finally managed to crack a weak smile. I went to bed and read in Lee Wulff's book about how much fun and what glorious sport salmon fishing is. Maybe he has something. I might just try it tomorrow.

*It is a delightful and bountiful planet in an unbelievably wonderful universe that man is privileged to inhabit. It is sad to realize that, because of the inequities existent within our socio-economic structure, only a fragment of the populace is in a position to appreciate, and to revel in what should be the glorious actuality of merely being alive. Relatively few are so situated that they can thrill to their participation in the magnificence and validity of the universe. This would seem to me to be the greatest of all tragedies—to exist but to be unable to glory in it. The rapture of living should be at the core of every individual's sojourn on Earth. There can be no tragedy in dying if, in living, having loved with all the heart.*

# 14

# Departure

I awoke this morning with the sad realization that today will be my last on the Pleasant for this year. I may run on down to New Brunswick to wind up the salmon season on the Miramichi, and it is quite possible I shall take more fish during the week there than I have throughout the past three months on the Pleasant, but it will be anticlimactic. Indeed, the trip will be taken largely to ease this parting with my favorite stream and its valley, the alternative abrupt transition, directly from here to the city, being just too hard to take.

My thoughts did not turn at once to salmon this morning. As a matter of fact, I felt disinclined to spend the whole day fishing. Instead, I wanted to drink in, all at once, as much of the river, its valley and inhabitants as I could and to store them away as a reservoir of memories to draw upon through the long winter months. Although well aware of the impossibility of swallowing up a whole river valley in a single gulp, I felt a compulsion to do my best, and so it was that I cooked breakfast before dawn, deep in the woods by the river, and then drove up to the hilltops of the western rim to watch the sunrise.

A sinuous bank of mist hung over the river below me, like a monstrous gray serpent lying asleep in a cradle of spruces. I drove on past the farmhouse on Luther Sawyer's land and dropped halfway down the hillside. Here I stopped and waited for the first rays of the sun to find the valley floor. I should then get a glimpse of the river itself, as gradually the mist burned off. It was all so quiet, so full of hushed peace. The blueberry harvest was over, the valley deserted.

The summer past, and all of those other summers, raced through my mind. What was not before my eyes I could still visualize, clearly, nostalgically, each bend and glide, rapids, pitch, and pool, from far up in the hills down to the distant sea, the golden sunny days, the summer showers, the birds, flowers, trees, insects, mink, deer, beaver, bear, the sights and sounds and odors, the people, the barrens, the forests, springs, brooks, rocks, trails, bridges.

Why is not this stream and its valley just that and nothing more? It is not that my acquaintance with rivers has been limited—I have waded hundreds, from coast to coast and from border to border. Why does this one small river mean so much? It has been niggardly in the salmon it has yielded compared with some other streams I have known. Its environs are neither so wild nor so tame

# Departure

as dozens I have wandered in. There is no one thing about it that stands out as conspicuously different, or as especially entrancing.

Actually, it is mediocre, almost insignificant, as rivers go, and its sparsely populated valley is not sprinkled with prosperous and productive farms and thriving communities—it is shabby and poor. The passerby sees nothing to stop for. Tourists never tarry here; indeed nowadays they whizz across the river without ever noticing it, over the new highway and bridge that by-pass the Village altogether, so that even the Village, the heart of the countryside, is seen by few others than those who still, for some reason that is not too clear, make it their home, while it slowly dwindles and withers, little by little, and sleeps and dreams of those other days when sawmills were busily whining away and furs were readily turned into dollars, ships were a-building, lobsters and fish abundant, and farm produce in demand. It is difficult to make a case for its continuation today, and one wonders how long it will be before it becomes only a ghost, its mission fulfilled, a tattered remnant of the past, no longer needed, discarded and left behind to decay in its dimming dreams and to sink back into the enveloping arms of the forest that patiently waits close by.

Truly, I find it impossible to account for my affection for the Pleasant. Not for its few salmon, certainly, and since I know more beautiful streams and more attractive surroundings, it is not just for its scenery either. What it is, frankly, eludes me, and it is futile, I think, to keep on trying to analyze my reactions to it in any attempt to explain its subtle significance. Rather, I will just accept it and my response to it and neither know nor care why. Some things are better left unanalyzed. There is always the possibility that penetrating insight might dilute or destroy the enchantment, whereas the unresolved mystery may serve constantly to whet it. I am not sure that this makes any sense or that it would withstand the objective attack of logic, but I am sure that I do not care either.

There must be Pleasant Rivers everywhere, if one chooses to seek them out. Actually, I am often uncertain about which river I refer to, confused between the Pleasant and pleasant rivers of my life; they merge, their currents seemingly plaited together to form a single stream at times, then divide around some islet only to rejoin beyond it.

I think of the friends I have in this valley and how much they mean to me and that I will not see them for a long time. I would like to stay, to go through winter evenings in their company, while snow lies deep in the valley and drifts across the roads and the Pleasant is locked fast under the ice.

This I cannot do. I can, however, even while sitting at my desk or working in my laboratory back there in the city, think about the snapping turtle buried deep in the mud of the river bottom, torpid, the feeble pulse and sluggish circulation maintaining the little spark that barely distinguishes life from death. The chub, dace, trout, and salmon slowly finning in the darkness of the deeper pools under a ceiling of ice and snow; the larvae of May flies, dragonflies, damsel flies, the water beetles, lurking in the cold ooze. I can visualize the brittle skeletons of the deciduous trees standing naked against the somber spruces and hear them crack with cold in the frigid night. The deer will be gathered in the winter yards, the bear snoozing away in his retreat, the beavers and muskrats snug in their lodges. The avian summer visitors will have long since

# Departure

departed, leaving storm-torn, snow-capped nests behind, now exposed where heretofore they lay unsuspected behind the screening foliage. The winter residents will have taken over—evening and pine grosbeaks, crossbills, snow buntings, snowy owls, perhaps a gyrfalcon. Seeds and bulbs will appear completely lifeless externally but, if carefully pried open, will reveal that wee virile speck of green, the embryonic magical perfection of adult form in miniature.

All of these living things waiting; waiting for the sun to climb high overhead once more and to send its probing rays of warmth and stimulation into every icy corner, to swing back the great cold door of winter and to allow spring to rush into the valley.

The toll of winter will be staggering. The dull, the slow, the stupid, the frail, the crippled, the sick, the unlucky will die. Only the fit and lucky will survive to know the quickening passion of spring's exciting caress and then the pulses will become swift and strong and there will be a great stirring and awakening, a bursting forth, a rebirth, an exuberation, an exultation, an ecstasy of resurgence, a breaking out, an escaping; and all through the valley there will be a creeping and crawling and wriggling and squirming, a finning and flying, running and bounding, a luxuriating and a growing and blossoming.

I can only hope that I shall be among the lucky and that I may be on hand to participate in the rhapsody of springtime, when I, too, may be reborn in the valley of the Pleasant.

I cannot stay to share winter with the valley's inhabitants. There is that other life I lead with another me, but Roger will write to keep me posted on events so that my detachment will not be complete and absolute. The slender strings will stretch over the miles between us, maintaining the bond, but with the coming of spring I shall be impatient to rush back as quickly as I can and, on my first visit, must scurry up and down the valley, seeing every thing and every person as speedily as possible, catching up on all that has transpired with river and people, all of it, greedily, eagerly, joyously.

And so, today, my major business is to say good-by. I will cast some flies, also, because I could not appropriately bid farewell to some of my favorite pools and runs in any other way. There are some places I shall go, merely to sit and look, not thinking so much as feeling—the deep-down-inside kind of feeling, I mean. There are faces to look into, hands to grip, without there being anything adequate to say.

I will slide the canoe into the river and paddle up it, through a certain stretch of quiet water, only to drift slowly down again, accomplishing nothing tangible or explainable but nevertheless something quite necessary. When the sun sinks low behind the spruces, I shall cook my supper on the shingle of sand opposite the Spring Brook and, when it is quite dark, I shall leave the valley. I could stay, sleeping again beside the river, but I find the parting somewhat easier in darkness than in daylight.

So, I must be off and about my business. This will be a day chock-full, from before dawn until after dark; and I shall have to hurry to meet all of my appointments, to complete my meandering rounds. This pause on the hillside was an essential part of my over-all leave-taking commitments. It was important to watch the day arrive in the valley and to indulge myself in some admittedly profitless reflections and meditations, though it has left me with but little time to spare before the sun shall have crossed over the valley and allowed night to close in upon the Pleasant. I shall then

# Departure

leave it like a treasured volume that I am sorry to have finished reading, though it has been read for the umpteenth time, and, having gleaned from it all I could in the rereading, close it only in hopes of opening its covers again and again in the years to come.